THERE WAS A CROOKED MAN, HE FLIPPED A CROOKED HOUSE

DAVID ERIK NELSON

First published in *The Magazine of Fantasy & Science Fiction*, July–August 2017

Cover art by Nicholas Grunas, ©2017

THERE WAS A CROOKED MAN, HE FLIPPED A CROOKED HOUSE

IT STARTED with this crooked house the Butcher Man bought sight unseen.

The "Butcher Man" I'm talking about is Felix Fleischermann, not his dad. Old Man Fleischermann, he'd been the original Butcher Man, the *real* Butcher Man, so called because he could "squeeze a dime out of every cut, even the squeal." With the passing of the Original Butcher Man we were left with the Butcher Man, Jr. Like a lot of sequels, he just wasn't as good. Butcher Man, Jr., had his moments: snatch up an abandoned property at $5,000, score a grant from Housing and Urban Development to rehab it, get back taxes waived because he's doing "blight reduction"; me and Lennie'd clear it, do some light repair, and it'd turn out to be an easy $30k flip. Detroit, arising from the ashes, et cetera, et cetera, et cetera. Unfortunately, those were more the exception than the rule for our Butcher Man, and you could tell that ate at him. He just wasn't his dad.

But that crooked house, hidden away in a bombed-out neighborhood of collapsed turn-of-the-century brick Tudors and stone French Renaissance Revivals, it was like finding a golden ticket tucked into all that Detroit rubble.

"Neat!" Lennie enthused as I rolled the little Chevy S-10 up to the ragged curb.

With his shaved head, beefy shoulders, and wrap-around Oakley Razors, Lennie looked like a Billy Badass downriver scrapper. Couldn't be further from the truth, though: Lennie is a learning-disabled thirty-year-old who lives in a group home in the suburbs. His greatest goal in life is to go to a Tigers game, a Lions game, and a Red Wings game all in one day. I've explained countless times that this is an impossible dream, but he dreams it none-theless, because it would be "Basically the best day, Glenn. Basically." I had the notion that the only reason Fleischermann kept Lennie around was that Lennie's mom and the Original Butcher Man had grown up together, back when the northside was nothing but Jews and black doctors. My own dad—Dr. Washington, son of Dr. Washington—had grown up on the northside, too. But by the time Dad hit Mumford High, all the Fleischermanns and Dorfmans and Epsteins had white-flown the coop, arising from the ashes, et cetera, et cetera.

"Neat," Lennie repeated, less sure of himself. "Right, Glenn?"

I climbed out for a better look.

The lot itself was a standard-issue Detroit trash heap: mounds of cracked brick, plastic bags snapping in the breeze, a curb-stomped shopping cart, a couple bizarrely healthy ghetto palms. But if you gave the house a second glance, the details popped out like red nail polish on an elephant.

Three stories, red stone exterior, high slate roof, cupola and tower, big curved bay window—the sort of European knock-offs Albert Kahn built for bankers and newspaper magnates when he first came to Detroit. But this one wasn't slumped precariously as a drunk in the kitchen doorway. Even on that heap of rubble, this house stood tall.

The steeply pitched roof was sound, as was that

conical turret. Those damned things almost never stood the test of time. But this one had. The whole place had. Not a single dangling shingle or cracked windowpane. Even the ornate front door, set into its shadowy little niche, stood unmolested: dark wood frame dominated by a diamond grid of dozens of flashing postage-stamp-sized leaded panes. No cages, no storms, no iron grate, and yet all damn near pristine.

Those windows—a couple were stained glass—that lovely old door, there was an easy couple grand in architectural antiques there for the motivated man with a Sawzall and enough extension cord. Not to mention everything inside: switch plates, fixtures, doorknobs, mirrors, the thick old copper wiring, the copper pipe, the iron radiators and cast-iron bathtubs. Sure, all that was harder to hock now than it had been a few years back, but it wasn't like this old girl showed up last week. She was an easy hundred years old, sitting in a neighborhood that had been bombed out for at least thirty of those years.

Lennie looked from me to the house, then back to me, studiously reading the expression on my face, keeping his own blank until he'd sorted out what I might be thinking. Then he broke into a wide grin.

"The Butcher Man sure can pick 'em!" he said. "*Amiright?*"

"You are right," I agreed absent-mindedly, then began to pick my way across the rubble-strewn lot. Now that I was moving, I saw that the house wasn't as perfect as I'd thought. It looked a little . . . I dunno. Slanted, but not quite slanted: the turret was straight, the chimney plumb, the doors and windows aligned and square in their frames, but none of the elements seemed quite square to each other. Focus on one piece and it all looked fine. But when you let your focus soften to take it all in at once, it slipped nauseatingly crooked.

Nonetheless, like every other black asshole in the first fifteen minutes of a horror film, I kept right on cruising toward the creepy abandoned house. I peeked through all those little glass panes in the front door and my heart leapt: the crooked house was fully furnished, in period, immaculate as a dollhouse.

"Hey! Lennie!" I shouted, my eyes never leaving the

interior. "C'mere with some flashlights! We *gotta* go in."

"Sure thing!" he honked. Behind me, I heard the S-10's springs groan and scream as Lennie hauled himself up into the bed to paw through the lock-box. I cupped my hands against the leaded glass and peered in. Despite the gloom of the day, it was reasonably bright in the old place. There was a short, dark-paneled entryway. On the right, a stairway swooped up and out of view. On the left, a wide arch doorway opened to a sitting room, complete with blue-velvet settee loveseat and all the walnut scrollwork a man could want. The walls were hidden behind dark floor-to-ceiling bookshelves still loaded with volumes. Further down the front hall there was another room lost in shadows—a dining room, I assumed—and past that a bright, sunny kitchen.

I glanced down to the doorknob, expecting to see one of those dangling KeyGuard push-button lockboxes, keys stowed inside. Realtors love those damn things. But there was no lockbox, and no doorknob—at least, not where I expected, along the left edge. Instead it was one of those queer-ass setups where the knob is centered.

THERE WAS A CROOKED MAN, HE FLIPPED A CROOKE...

But still no lockbox. Usually it wouldn't matter: half of Butcher Man, Jr.'s buys didn't even have a front door, and the other half you'd just as well pop the fucker off her hinges with a pry bar. That was Lennie's specialty.

But there was no way in hell I was giving this lady that treatment. I'd sooner use a crowbar on my dear old grandma than on that beautiful door.

"Lennie!" I called over my shoulder. "Lennie, Imma need my lockpicks out of the glove box, too!"

And that's when the patrol car squawked its siren.

Given a big white guy and a little black guy, folks always assume the white guy's in charge, even if that white guy is obviously mentally challenged.

Always. Because folks are racist.

And that goes double if the folks are cops. Fat cops, skinny cops, cops who climb on rocks; black cops, white cops, even cops with chicken pox—

are racist. Across the board and without exception.

Just my opinion, but "*post-racial America*"? My black ass.

I raised my hands and turned, slow and

7

nonthreatening as a fluffy white cloud on a sunny day. The cops were already out of their prowler. Cop A was talking to Lennie. He had dark Malcolm X glasses and a tight fade, although not tight enough to eliminate all the gray salting his temples. Cop B—the one who'd leaned in to flick the siren and rollers—was a younger guy, clean-shaven and clear-eyed, hand on the butt of his sidearm. Both cops were black like me. I had no delusions about that making shit easier.

I heard Cop A tell Lennie, "Get your man over here."

Lennie turned, cupping his big hands around his mouth: "Hey, Glenn! Th—"

"Yeah. Yeah." I waved him off with one of my raised hands as I jogged down the steps. "I heard. I heard. We do not consent to a search, officers."

"Who said anything about a search?" Cop B asked, still standing by the cruiser, watchful, ready to draw and take cover.

"I did," I said. "In that we do not consent to one."

Cop A was asking Lennie for his driver's license.

Lennie—who doesn't have one and, God willing, never will—stitched his brow.

"You don't have to give him ID, Lennie," I said. "You don't have to talk to them."

"I don't drive," Lennie said uncertainly to Cop A.

"We don't consent to a search," I repeated.

Cop A, in the Malcolm X specs, smiled. "What are you, a lawyer? No one said anything about a search. But we'd like to look in your vehicle, sir." This last he said to Lennie, which infuriated me all over again.

"I, um, I do not consent to a search?" Lennie said uncertainly, eyes on me.

"Don't look at him," Cop A told Lennie, "look at me, sir. Look at me. I am asking *you* if I can look in *your* vehicle. You let the lawn boy boss you around?" Cop A clearly wasn't grokking Lennie's constitutional inability to get rattled by subtle jabs at his masculinity. "Who *is* in charge here?"

Lennie and I spoke simultaneously. Lennie said, "We're both in charge!" I said, "I am."

Lennie was visibly hurt.

Cop A rolled his eyes.

"We're looking in the vehicle. *You*—" he pointed at me "—are going to produce a driver's license, 'cause this truck got here somehow, and *you*—" he pointed at Lennie "—are going to give me a name my partner can look up—"

"We do *not* consent to any—" I began.

"And *you*—" he pointed at me again "—are going to shut up about not consenting to any search. You two gentlemen were skulking around private properties and loudly discussing a B 'n' E when we arrived. We have probable cause, you're both detained, and you're going to sit tight while I look to see if you do indeed have burglar's tools and/or stolen property in the vehicle, as per your conversation easily heard from the public thoroughfare."

I was out of my depth. These scenarios went a lot smoother in those "Know Your Rights!" YouTube videos.

"Listen," I told Cop A in my most reasonable voice, stepping closer and dropping my hands, "we're not consenting—"

And then I was in the greasy dirt, my face against the cracked curb, clean-cut Cop B cuffing me.

"Yikes!" Lennie shouted.

"Your chauffeur is fine," Cop A told Lennie. "Full name, sir?"

Cop B hauled me up by my elbows and planted my ass on the broken curb. "License?" he said, just as casually.

"Glove box," I replied. "In my wallet."

Cop B smiled. "So, then I presume that you consent—"

"Yeah, yeah." I refused to look at him. Out in the hazy distance I could see the tall towers of the Renaissance Center perched at the river's edge, standing dominion over all.

"Leonard Epstein," Lennie was telling Cop A. "E-P-S-T-E-I-N."

Cop A raised an eyebrow and gave Lennie the visual once-over: the big hands and shoulders, the height, the shaved head, the Billy Badass wrap-arounds. "Funny," Cop A said, "you don't look like an *Epstein.*"

Lennie was agog at this. "You know my folks?"

Cop A smirked, and then his features clouded. You could actually watch it all come together in his head: the beefy dumbbell with the weirdly unmodulated voice, wide-open face, and no driver's license. Not even an asshole cop wants to see himself as the kind of asshole that clowns on a learning-disabled dude.

"Yeah," Cop A said crisply. "Nice people. Good Americans."

Meanwhile, Cop B had found the truck's registration, my wallet, my lockpicks—and beneath that the Ziploc bag with my surety bond and intermediate certificate from the Associated Locksmiths of America.

"I'm a card-carrying member," I announced. Michigan doesn't license locksmiths, but if you're a black man whose livelihood includes jimmying doors, you sure as shit best go out of your way to make yourself indubitably legit. "Membership card's in the wallet," which Cop B was already riffling as he walked back to his cruiser.

Cop A called over to his partner, who had just started typing at the laptop bolted to their dashboard. "This vehicle registered to an Epstein or—?" He cocked his head at me.

"Washington," Cop B supplied, "Glenn. No priors, no warrants, no outstanding tickets, no middle name. Vehicle is registered to 'Fleischermann and Fleischermann Properties, LLC.'"

Cop A shifted his attention back to Lennie. "Who are the Fleischermanns?"

"Our boss," Lennie supplied eagerly, and then frowned, "and his dad, of blessed memory. Mr. Fleischermann, the alive one, bought this house, and we're here to check it out and figure if it's a fixer-upper or a tearer-downer."

"That so?" Cop A asked. It struck me as odd that he continued sizing Lennie up instead of looking at the house. "But he didn't give you keys?"

"Usually they're in a lockbox on the doorknob," Lennie offered. Again, the cop didn't even glance at the house. It was as if he already knew that he wouldn't see any lockbox dangling from the knob. "These keys must be lost. That happens sometimes, but it doesn't matter because Glenn's a fully bonded locksmith with an intermediate certificate from the Associated Locksmiths of America."

"You have *no* keys for this property?" Cop A confirmed.

"Yup," Lennie nodded.

"Hence the lockpicks?"

"Yup!"

Cop A nodded once, satisfied.

Cop B climbed out of his cruiser. "Epstein, Leonard, is clear," he announced as he sauntered over to the curb where I was sitting. Lennie beamed like he'd won a spelling bee. "Washington, Glenn, is clear, too." He dropped my wallet and papers next to my boots. "Vehicle is not reported stolen, insurance is current, surety bond is valid. Stand up."

I struggled to stand—it's hard to do if you're a chubby guy sitting on busted-up curb with your hands chicken-winged behind you. Cop B waited, then gestured for me to turn around. He uncuffed me and returned to his cruiser without a word.

Cop A gave us each the once-over once more, then tossed a, "Carry on, fellas," over his shoulder as he climbed back into the cruiser. I rubbed my wrists as they pulled off. Lennie waved like a kid at a parade.

"Can you believe Officer Jones knows my folks?" He meant Cop A.

"Yeah, it's a small world after all." I stooped to pick up my papers. "When'd you get his name?"

"*Duh*, Glenn—it was on his name tag. Officers Jones and Washington. Hey!" He turned to me. "Are you and Officer Washington related?"

I feigned annoyance. "That's racist, Lennie," I said solemnly.

Lennie's jaw dropped.

"No! Glenn! I didn't mean it like that! There's lot of black people that aren't related! I just meant because you're both named Washington—"

I chuckled. My wrists hurt and I was almost terminally annoyed, but Lennie has a good heart, and that always puts me in a good mood.

"I'm just fucking with you, Lennie."

"Gle-eeeeen!" Lennie shouted in delight, snorting a laugh. "Wheaton's Law, Glenn!" By which Lennie meant *Don't be a dick!*—but without having to "cuss."

"OK, OK. Let's get to work." I leaned through the truck window, shoved the papers back in the glove box, and snatched up my picks. "Get the flashlights and come check this shit out."

Up on the porch, Lennie was suitably impressed.

"Neat!" he said, his voice muffled by the glass just an inch from his moist mouth. "See, I told you the Butcher Man could pick 'em."

"Even a stopped clock is right twice a day, Len."

"Mr. Fleischermann has a clock that's right all the time," Lennie said, still peering through the diamond-grid of tiny jewel-like panes. "It calibrates every hundred milliseconds to the National Institute of Standards and Technology's NIST-F2 atomic clock in Boulder, Colorado, through its very own Internet cable, Glenn. It even does Daylight Savings time all by itself." I let this bout of "Lennisplaining" wash over me, because I'd heard it roughly one jigeddy-jillion times. I'm nearly positive it was the verbatim marketing copy off the manufacturer's website. He had similar spiels on the iPad Retina Display ("264 to 326 pixels-per-inch, Glenn!") and his parents' thermostats ("sensor-driven, Wi-Fi-enabled, self-learning, programmable thermostats and smoke detectors produced by Nest Labs of Palo Alto, California, Glenn!")

"That's swell, Len. Step back so I can pop her."

Lennie stepped aside obligingly and I peered at the lockset. That centered knob was pretty old but the cylinder relatively new, a bump-proof six-pin Schlage core with a reversed keyway. Whoever put this bad boy in was serious about that door staying locked—which was kinda funny with all that antique glass. A big boy like Lennie could have pushed his way in without breaking a sweat.

But none of that was in my head right then; I just wanted to open that door and get a clear look into that sitting room. Most of me was totally realistic that this was gonna be one of those Georges Seurat situations: looks great from a distance, but close up you see that it only looked good because your brain was filling in the gaps with *a lot* of wishful thinking.

The lock popped in short order—those Schlage cylinder plugs are solid and worth the money, but they're strictly for thwarting YouTube dilettantes with bump keys, not fully bonded and certified members of the ALA like myself.

I turned the knob left, then right, the door stuck for a second, then swung in to the right—which isn't what I'd expected. Hanging the door that way awkwardly blocked the stairs and entryway. You'd have assumed it'd open to the left, where it could lie flush against the wall. For a second, I wondered if this odd decision had been the original architect's, or if some later occupant had rehung it and fucked up the entryway flow for their own dumbass reasons.

The door swung clear, giving us our first unobstructed look inside.

"Wow!" Lennie gasped in my ear. "It's perfect!"

That was an understatement. The place was immaculate: a bright sunbeam cut down through the high stained-glass windows at the landing halfway up the staircase, throwing fiery color on the iridescent Pewabic tiles lining the foyer. There were no puddles, no drifts of leaves, no midden-piles from squatters, no musty smell, not even mouse poops. I've lived in the wilds of the D for years and most places, if you leave your joint for a long weekend, you're gonna come home to find poops on your counter and in the corners. The Motor City mouse simply hustles harder than any other mouse in the world.

But this joint was spotless. And scentless: no mildew or rot or garbage, but also none of the good smells of old wood oil or antique books or mellow, ancient fireplace smoke. No nothing.

I started through the doorway, then stumbled, even though the porch and entryway were flush, without so much as a thick threshold. I heard a door clap shut behind me and found myself on my knees in the backyard, nothing before me but dirt, rubble, and the distant Detroit skyline against a flat, gray sky. Somewhere Lennie was shouting his head off. I turned around and was looking at the back of the crooked house. There was a shallow screen porch with a wood-framed door tacked onto its back. Three wooden steps led down to the yard, where I crouched.

"I'm back here, Lennie!" I hollered, finding my feet. "Come join me!" I heard Lennie's workboots crunching through the rubble, and a second later he popped around the corner.

"Glenn!" he shouted. "How'd you get back here?"

"Back door," I said, nodding toward the screen porch.

"But—"

"Wait here for a sec, *right* here. Don't move an inch. Don't take your eyes off the screen door."

"Yeah. OK," Lennie said, his eyes locked on the door.

I jogged around the house and up the front steps, my heart still racing, but not with fear. I was pumped. Standing in the open front doorway, toes to the threshold and eyes on that bright sitting room, I took a deep breath and yelled: "Lennie!"

"What?"

"I'm on the stoop!"

"OK?"

And then I leapt through paratrooper style, ankles and knees together and loose, ready to roll if necessary. I banged right through the back screen door and landed at the bottom of the steps, both feet solid, sticking a perfect-ten dismount.

The screen door clattered closed behind me.

All at once I understood why there were no leaves or puddles or mouse droppings, why in contrast to the rest of the City of Detroit, this place could still have nice things.

"Call Fleischermann," I said breathlessly, my heart racing, eyes roving over the house. I wanted to hug the place. I wanted to dive through again and again and again. *Oh, what the hell?* I thought, jogged up the three wooden steps, and pulled open the screen door.

That narrow, tacked-on screen porch was more or less as tidy as foyer: a little pile of leaves blown in one corner, but otherwise clean and orderly. Dim. A snow shovel leaned against the house's red block wall. The back door was closed but the curtained window glowed, Norman Rockwell-style.

I took one big step through the portal. And my boot clomped down on the boards, sending me stumbling against the house's back wall. I hadn't expected that. I reached out to the back door— another of those center-set knobs—but it wouldn't budge. I don't know why, but I pressed my ear to the window glass, held my breath, and listened.

The room beyond was silent, of course. I had the lock open in two quick rakes. The door swung in, revealing a kitchen straight out of one of those Detroit Historical Museum displays: four-burner enameled range, deep two-tub sink, Hoosier cabinet, icebox instead of a fridge. All of it pin-neat: no leaves. No mouse turds. I stepped in, tumbled, and fell on my ass as the linoleum floor angled away beneath me. The kitchen was gone, the ceiling replaced with gray skies, the floor tilted, no longer flat rolled lino but instead slanted roofing slates.

I slid down the steeply pitched roof on my ass, flailing. One hand blindly grabbed at the window ledge behind me and held on for dear life. I hung there for a second, eyes clamped shut, enveloped in the metallic summertime tang of damp slates, copper gutters, and warm tar. My lockpicks tingled and clattered down the roof, then off the edge.

Somewhere far below, Lennie shouted, "Ow! Hey! Gle-eeen! What gives?"

I opened my eyes. My hands were clamped around the dark wood sill of a little top-hung window on the side of the turret. I was through that window

in a heartbeat, not giving a moment's considera-
tion to what I might land on when I hauled myself
back in.

But instead of landing in a hot, musty attic, I found
myself flopping onto the hard slab of the front
stoop.

"Mr. Fleischermann is coming," Lennie called from
the front yard. I sat up.

"What'd you tell him?"

Lennie was standing on the broken pavers of the
front walk, rubbing his head where the lockpicks
had clonked him.

"That it was important. That you popped the door
but couldn't get inside. And that we'd met those
nice police that know my folks. And that you
couldn't talk 'cause you were maybe on the roof.
And then he said not to move 'cause he was
coming and he hung up."

Part of me wanted to keep messing with those
doors, to see if they always led to the same places,
to see if there were any other doors or windows I
could pop and pass through, to see what happened
if I just shoved my arm in, hokey-pokey style. But

my better angels knew we were pressing our luck already.

I stood and dusted off. "Let's find my picks." Lennie held up the folded leather case. I jogged down the steps to check it.

"There's a couple missing. Where did it land?"

Lennie pointed around to the side of the house, but didn't follow as I started over.

"C'mon," I cajoled, "help me look."

"But Mr. Fleischermann told me not to move, Glenn."

"He just meant not to leave the property. C'mon. I can't open shit without my S-rake."

Lennie looked dubious but came along. We found the S-rake and L-rake almost immediately, but were still looking for my snowman pick and twist-flex tension wrench when Fleischermann babied his cobalt-blue Jaguar up to the crumbling curb.

"Leonard!" he shouted from the curb. "What the fuck? You said you were on the front walk, and I said not to move, and I get here, and you're fucking around in the rock garden with Glenn."

"Glenn dropped—"

"I said, 'Don't move, Leonard!' What the fuck, Leonard?"

Lennie glowered at me. "I told you," he mumbled as he moped over to where Fleischermann stood in his immaculate blue suit, hands on hips.

It turned out Lennie had been standing on both my twist-flex wrench and my snowman pick. I scooped them up and shoved them in my inside jacket pocket. When it comes to those cheap-ass wafer-tumbler locks—the kind on desks and file cabinets and garages—the snowman is the only pick for me. I could live without that particular tension wrench, but not without my snowman.

"What the fuck is this about the doors and the roof?" Fleischermann gazed past me, his small, sharp eyes inventorying the crooked house, scanning the gutters and windows, crawling across the block walls looking for ladder cracks and split lintels. "Was the roof good?" he asked, not looking away.

"I don't know," I said, "I was only up there for a few seconds."

"Leonard said you had trouble with the door. Door's wide open." He finally turned and stared at me, hard and keen. The Younger Fleischermann wasn't his dad but he was still cut from the same cloth. "What's the situation?"

"Come look," I said.

By the time we reached the bottom step, Fleischer-mann could see clearly through the door into that sunny parlor—and for the first time I thought to wonder where all that sunshine was coming from; the day was dishwater gray, the sky clogged with a blanket of low dryer-lint clouds. There was no sun to shine into that sitting room, let alone somehow throw bright beams perpendicular to each other, one straight in through the bay window, the other directly down the staircase.

Fleischermann whistled low as he mounted the front steps. "Jackpot," he said reverently, striding toward the threshold. Lennie caught his arm. Fleischermann glared at Lennie's grabbing hand and Lennie dropped him like he was hot.

"Hold up," I said, sliding past the Butcher Man, careful our shoulders didn't touch. "Check this out." I thrust my arm through the doorway.

Nothing happened. Mr. Fleischermann looked at me in bewildered annoyance.

"Guess you gotta put your whole self in," I said lamely, then squared my shoulders and leapt. The world went bright, then black, the wood-framed screen door slammed open, and I landed squarely in the backyard. Behind me the screen door creaked, then clapped shut.

"Fuckin' A!" Fleischermann exclaimed from the front porch. "Mother. Fucker."

Then he tumbled out the screen door himself, teetered on the topmost of the three wooden steps, and came pinwheeling down. I shocked us both by stepping up and catching him in a big bear hug, saving that fine suit the indignity of a dirt bath.

I thought he'd be pissed I was touching him, but instead Fleischermann patted me on the back. "Thank you, Glenn," he said with no trace of pique. We stepped away from each other. He didn't make eye contact, instead fussing with his suit, shaking his head as he did so. "You stumble on a job site, scrape your palms, and the next thing you know you're on a respirator because of some antibiotic-resistant bullshit."

Which is how Fleischermann, Sr.—the Original Butcher Man, hard as a mouthful of sixpenny nails —had gone out, flattened by a raging MRSA infection he picked up when he stumbled while checking out a property he ultimately decided wasn't worth buying anyway. Young Fleischermann finished fussing with his suit, smoothed his dark hair, and then turned, mounted the back steps, opened the screen door, and peered in, careful that no part of him crossed the threshold. The back door stood open still.

"You did that?" he asked, indicating the open door.

"Yup."

"And you can't get in that way, either?"

"Nope. Puts you on the roof."

He turned to look at me, eyebrow cocked. "The roof?"

"Yup."

"And from the roof?"

"I climbed in the little window on the turret."

"And . . . ?"

"Wound up back on the front stoop."

I was expecting a little enthusiasm, if not gratitude. But Fleischermann cursed under his breath. He stood there, looking like a guy who's run the numbers in his head for the tenth time and confirmed that he does indeed have absolutely no way to pay both the electric and cable bills this month.

The Butcher Man came down the steps shaking his head. He walked around to the front, and I followed.

"It does that every time?" he asked, frowning, his eyes scanning the side of the house as he passed.

"Yeah."

We were back at the front walk, standing shoulder to shoulder, looking at the open front door.

"Well, *fuck*." He sighed. "This went from dandy to dog shit in record time."

"You had no clue this place was, um . . ." I faltered, then came up with, "*Special?*"

Fleischermann turned and looked at me like I was an idiot. His face worked oddly as he processed through a string of emotions—wonder, annoyance, offense, shame, then something akin to grief—before settling on anger. Then he unloaded with both barrels.

"Yeah, Glenn, fucking shockingly, I had no fucking notion that I was paying cash money for the only red-stone French Revival in Detroit that's *also* a fucking Möbius strip!" His voice quickly got shrill. "The buyer's always the last to fucking know, right?"

"No, no," I said, hands raised placatingly, "I just meant the *condition*, that it's so well preserved, fully furnished!"

"Of course it's fucking fully furnished, Glenn!" Fleischermann shouted. "No one can get in to loot the fucker!" Lennie had drawn back to Fleischermann's Jag, hands covering his ears. "I've bought a beautiful house you can't go into on a piece of land that's less than worthless embedded in a fucking necrotic abscess on the diabetic ass of the most notoriously moribund city in North fucking America, Glenn! We can't even fucking strip it for the copper and doorknobs!"

I was getting hot under the collar by then but I

didn't know why. "Are you looking?" I asked. "This is a beautiful piece of architecture *and* it is a magic-ass house, Fleischermann! You go in one door, you come out another without visiting any of the places in between! And it ain't symmetrical! You can't go back the way you came! Lots of houses got granite countertops and good schools, but how many houses got *that*? That's *gotta* be worth *something*!"

"To who?" Fleischermann asked. His voice was a dark, dead-level rumble, his face clouded like tornado skies. "For what?"

And I had no fucking clue.

"It's like a teleporter—" I ventured.

"That teleports between the front door and back door of a house that's someplace no one in their right mind wants to be. Get a clue, shit-wit: just because something is *rare*, that doesn't make it *valuable*."

I was literally speechless. Fleischermann had seen the problem immediately, while I'd been totally hoodwinked by the gee-whiz: the house did an amazing thing that was absolutely useless.

"You could open a Mystery Spot," Lennie hazarded from the end of the front walk. "There's lots of parking around here."

Fleischermann rolled his eyes up to the heavens, then covered them with one hand.

"Yeah, Leonard, but where would we put the go-cart track and Putt-Putt?"

Lennie looked around, surveying the adjacent lots. "Hmmmm," he began. "Weeeeel, if you cleared these two and graded them—"

I cut him off.

"Just because we don't know what it's useful for, that doesn't mean it's useless," I said. "Someone will pay for a thing like this—like the University of Michigan or Wayne State. Or the government."

Fleischermann sighed at my naïveté, shoulders slumped. "Leonard," he called out, "you know Dick Schnabel?"

"Yeah!" Lennie said. "He used to come to my parents' New Year's party when I was little." Lennie's face grew solemn. "He's a serious dude."

Fleischermann chuckled and, for a moment, he *was*

his dad. "That he is, Leonard. Dick Schnabel is a serious, serious dude. And Dick Schnabel had a Moon rock. A little one. It's a long story, and I know I'd fuck up some details, but the gist is his dad—Hersch Schnabel, of blessed memory—knew this electrical engineer who'd worked for NASA and palled around with Armstrong and Aldrin and them. This engineer was a timid little nebbish, and those big swinging NASA dicks thought he was a scream, so they sorta adopted him, like a mascot. When he retired, one of them gave him a little chip of the Moon, which he kept in a test tube with a black rubber stopper. Dick's dad got it from the guy—I don't know how or for what—and Dick inherited it. I remember, when we were kids, Hersch Schnabel would open that test tube and let us take a sniff. Gunpowder. The fucking Moon smells like gunpowder, if you can fucking fancy that. Anyway, a couple years back, Dick decides he should get the thing authenticated and appraised, get a rider for it on his insurance. So he calls the fucking University of fucking Michigan, and they call NASA—or whoever—and the next thing Dick Schnabel knows, there are two special agents sitting in his reception area. Turns out, according to the Feds, *all* lunar material is government property. Doesn't matter if you bought it fair and square. Doesn't matter if you got it from a guy NASA gifted it to themselves. Doesn't matter if Neil Armstrong handed it to you with his own fucking hand. That shit is one hundred percent nontransferable, for ever and ever, *amen*."

Fleischermann turned and began ambling back down the walk toward his Jag, digging his keys out of his pocket.

"This isn't a Moon rock," I said lamely.

"It's something extra-special. Like a Moon rock," he replied breezily, "they'll take it, and I'll be out a hundred and thirty-seven grand."

My jaw dropped.

"You paid real-house money for a Detroit flipper?" A hundred thirty-seven grand wasn't much, but the economy of Southeast Michigan isn't much, either. A man could mos def get a tidy little house out in the suburbs, where they still had functional schools and trash pickup and snow removal, for a hundred and thirty-seven grand.

Fleischermann slowed. His jaw was set and he was staring at his keys, as though trying to puzzle out which was for what, like as though the big plastic Jaguar fob wasn't a clue. "It was a municipal thing," he said. "The house was a dollar, but you had to pay back taxes and liens and encumbrances and clear the title—" He looked at me, eyes blazing, color in his cheeks. "I don't know why I'm fucking explaining myself to the goddamn help. The point is, it fucking added up. And with everything and the legal fees, I'm in for $137,404.64."

"Why'd you buy it?" I asked, honestly curious.

He looked at the crooked house forlornly. The fire in his eyes had faded to ash. "Fucking MLS." He meant that Multiple Listing Service real estate brokers use to track the vitals on what's for sale by whom, for how much. "The listing for it said the architect was Quintus Teal."

"Who's Quintus Teal?"

"I've got no fucking clue. But when MLS says who the architect is, you figure it's a big deal. Like Albert Kahn. The abandoned Packard Plant would have got bulldozed sixty years ago, except that it's an Albert Kahn. One of Dad's rules: if they name the architect, then he's a BFD."

"So who's Quintus Teal? A big fucking deal?"

"A big fucking nobody. Fucker did this, then moved out to California, where he mostly did modernist and postmodern residential stuff."

"And those . . . ?"

"Ashes, ashes, they all fell down. Ages ago. This was a stupid buy, but when it was a stupid buy at five thousand, I wasn't so fucking lathered."

We turned back to stare at the perfect, crooked, impenetrable money pit. Fleischermann chewed his lower lip, his eyes again scanning the roof's peak—straight as the horizon—the chimney, the turret.

"Damn shame," he said. "Those slate roofs wear like iron, and those fucking turrets are a bitch to restore but that one looks damn near perfect. Bet it's fucking beautiful upstairs. Imagine the views from those windows, up on this little hill, with most of the rest of the neighborhood down. Somebody'd buy. Even here, somebody'd buy." He sighed. "Lennie said the cops were fucking with you?" He squinted as he said this, but his eyes never left the house.

I'd forgotten about the cops; it'd been a long morning. "Yeah."

"What the fuck were they doing out here in the middle of BFE?"

I looked around the bombed-out neighborhood again. The DPD motto is something like "Making Detroit a safer place to live, work, and visit." There sure as hell wasn't anyone living, working, or visiting up in here—except me and Lennie, and we were the ones they came to fuck with.

Fleischermann gave a final sigh. "What fucking ever. Mysteries within mysteries. Here." He held out a key ring with two keys on it. One was a shiny Schlage with *DO NOT DUPLICATE* stamped on it. The other was a cheap, bent wafer-tumbler key splotched with rust. I added them to the jangling "janitor's knot" clipped to my belt.

"Lock her up," Fleischermann said. "You and Leonard come back tomorrow, do something about the yard and our section of sidewalk, just in case the DPD plans to issue a bunch of bullshit 'community standards' citations." He grunted, rolling his eyes at the condition of the "community." "Then put up a fucking fence." He paused, eyed the house one last time, and frowned. "But don't go overboard," he added—i.e., he wanted us to cheap-out: a decent chain link gate over the walkway, but that orange plastic bullshit snow fencing for the rest. Both Fleischermanns chronically pulled penny-wise, pound-foolish bullshit like that.

And that was that. Turned out we didn't need the keys: the locksets' sprung latches automatically engaged when the doors were closed. Lennie and I did the work over a couple days, but I didn't mess with the magic doors any more; my wonder had soured—which is kind of a pattern for me. Present station notwithstanding, I'm the proud holder of a $111,000 B.Arch. Did my internship with Lowenstein|Ziegler. Designed a little yoga studio/coffee shop space and did everything but the engineering myself; custom built-ins, the works. The client was ecstatic. But that whole time, for me, it was like my light was dimming. It was a great job, I guess, but the day-to-day felt meaningless. When I was done, I didn't even bother taking the Architect Registration Exam to get my license. Much to Dr. Washington's chagrin, I was living in Detroit in a brownstone I'd bought at auction for pennies on the dollar, slowly restoring it, mouthing vague plans to rent out apartments, all the while sorta quietly waiting for the momentum to die on that, too.

A week or two after Lennie and I wrapped up I found myself in the Old Miami, chatting up this gal with a camera.

It was late afternoon. The Old Miami is one of those old-skool brick bomb shelter-looking bars down on Cass. It's the one with the green awning. It's a kinda trendy spot now and gets pretty rowdy late at night, but in the afternoon it is what it is: a grandpa bar.

I was sitting there nursing a non-ironic Pabst Blue Ribbon next to this College for Creative Studies student. She was studying "time-based media" and "the place of place in post-Information culture." I myself studied plain ole architecture at the Cranbrook Academy of Art, out in Detroit's bougiest suburb—but I didn't delude myself that this gal was drinking cut-rate on Cass Ave in order to find a dude with a meaningfully informed opinion of Le Corbusier (who, in my humble, is a moderately overrated genius inadvertently responsible for about 4/5ths of the fugly in modern American urban sprawl).

Her name was Anja. She had yardstick-straight, moth-wing blonde hair and one of those purring European accents where they end most sentences with *Já?* She was drinking Old Crow neat, and she smelled like oleander and fresh-cut grass. Sitting on the bar next to her glass was an honest-to-God 35mm Leica. True to stereotype, she was mad-crazy for the Fabulous Ruins of Detroit.

"I've made pictures at the Michigan Central Rail Station, *já?* And as well at Packard Plant, and also the highly ornamented parking structure that was the Detroit's Michigan's Theater, *já?*"

"*Já,*" I said.

"But those—" she frowned and made an obscure gesture "—they are like the . . . You see the sign along the road, and you go to take the picture of the thing that is famous because everyone takes the picture of that thing?"

"Tourist trap?" I offered, and her eyes sparkled.

"Yeeeees! Those places—the train station, the ornate parking of the Michigan's Building Theater —these are the tourist traps of Detroit." We both nodded and smiled, simpatico, and it hit me: I still had the keys to the crooked house on my key ring.

"Heeeey!" I said. "You wanna see something extra-special?"

Of course she did.

I downed my beer, she downed her fashionably bottom-shelf bourbon, and we were out the door.

Where she promptly laughed in my face.

"Ah," she said knowingly, eyeballing my saggy pickup in that lurid late-afternoon light, a ragged tarp and dirty shovel conspicuous in back. Straight-Up Ed Gein shit. Dammit. "Certainly," she chuckled, "I shall without second thought take a ride in the truck of a stranger for a late-afternoon tour of the wilds of 'extra-special' Detroit, *já?*" She was being playful, but was also being firm.

I laughed, too. "Don't worry, we can walk from here—it's closer than you'd think." Which is one of Detroit's charms: the fabulous ruins are *always* closer than you'd think.

She squinted at me, still smiling, clearly weighing the intense desire to be shown something extra-special against her mother's admonishments to be wary of dark strangers promising extra-special treatment.

"First I take your picture and text it to my friend,

tell her this is the man for the police to seek out if I do not return, *já?*"

"*Já*," I said, and offered a broad, toothy smile for the photo. "Hey, give her my name and number, too. Just in case she thinks I'm cute."

"Oh." She pouted. "But I have not these to give."

"Well, then, I'll furnish them." She smiled and typed my name and number into her text, hit send, and then highlighted the name and number and added me to her address book. I wanted to high-five myself.

We walked up Cass Avenue, then cut back into the bombed-out Victorian neighborhood. When we turned the corner she was immediately taken with the crooked house. In that fiery October light it was something to see, looming out of the blaze on its little hill.

"My," she said, raising her camera. *Click, whir.*

"You ain't seen nothing yet."

I advanced, waving her toward the gate. But it had a new lock. Lennie and I had used a four-digit all-season Master Lock ProSeries—which is a damn good lock. But it had been replaced with a blue

Master Lock Speed Dial in a rubber bumper—one of those "directional" padlocks with that joystick doohickey instead of a dial. Those are a damned pain in the ass: shock- and shim-resistant, and basically impossible to guess the combo on. The new lock tweaked me out a touch. Why the hell would Fleischermann swap the lock? And who the hell did he send out to swap it?

"We're gonna have to jump the fence," I announced.

Anja's eyes sparkled. She took three steps back and vaulted the chain link nimbly, like a gymnast dismounting the pommel horse. I hauled myself over with a good deal less grace, but her laughter was good-natured.

"Shall we?" I said, offering my arm. She finished snapping another pic.

"Indeed." She slipped her hand through the crook of my elbow.

"Excellent, madame. Follow me to the main event."

We mounted the front steps and I slipped the Schlage key into that centered knob. It turned easily.

"Perhaps," Anja said, "you shall carry me across the threshold?" That sounded rad, but I'm not a big dude, and I wasn't sure I wouldn't drop her when I abruptly came down the back steps.

The door swung in to the left, flush against the paneled interior wall. That looked wrong, but I didn't want to stop and think about it. Not right that second. Right that second, I wanted to show off.

I heard her breath catch when the door cleared the jamb, revealing first the dramatic sweep of the staircase, and then the flawlessly mellow sitting room. The savage light of the late sun fell across Anja's delicate face, sparking golden threads in her pale hair. *"Gud minn godur!"* she muttered, her pricy little antique Leica all but forgotten in her hand.

I grinned. "Check this shit out."

Then I stepped over the threshold. And my boot clomped heavily onto the entryway's Pewabic tiles.

It was my turn to be fucking gobsmacked: I was *in the house*. It slowly dawned on me that the door had opened the *opposite* way this time, swinging to the left and laying flat against the entryway wall instead of swinging awkwardly to the right. It likewise dawned on me that this was the first time I'd used the actual key to unlock the door.

"This is astounding," she said, stepping past me. "Whose home is this?"

"No one's," I said. "It's abandoned. My boss bought it to flip, but then . . ." I trailed off, because I'd lost the thread of my thoughts entirely. The house was beautiful. In the book-lined sitting room, the blue velvet settee stood between a side table with a green-glass-shaded library lamp and a blue wing-back chair with gold fringe. These faced a grand fireplace surrounded by more glowing Pewabic tile. The wall opposite the arched doorway was all built-in bookcases, too, save for a wide, cushioned window seat. The broad, dark windows showed us our own ghostly reflections. I took a deep breath and got a snootful of old woodsmoke and that vanilla-bourbon perfume of lots of old books, lovingly kept. It was the perfect, platonic ideal of "genteel Victorian white guy's parlor."

Anja had already crossed to the shelves. I steadied myself against the banister rail and stared down the back hall into the kitchen.

Something was wrong with the kitchen. Something was wrong with the house.

"These books," she said. "These must be jokes, *já?*"

I grunted something. The banister was cool and smooth under my palm. And wrong.

"The titles," she said, the smile draining from her voice, "these titles are very strange. Some are French, some Hebrew, many look as to be Esperanto. This one is Esperanto," she said, setting her finger on an ancient, flaking brown binding. "I believe it says it is the memoir of William Shatner. This one—" she set her finger on an unbroken spine in navy-blue and red with gold lettering "—it says *A Brief History of Time*, but the author is Warren G. Harding."

My mouth was dry, and it answered without my thinking. "Twenty-ninth President of the United States, born 1865, died 1923. Highest approval rating of any sitting US president ever." I won the Presidential Bee in 5th grade. We all have our little Lennisplaining moments, I guess.

Here was the first thing that was bothering me about the house: that banister under my hand was glossy and smooth, not dried or cracked. No dust. I could accept the lack of leaves and trash and vermin and mildewy stank—after all, until just now, nothing had been able to enter the house, including mice and leaves and rainwater. But even a locked room gets dusty, and a varnished handrail sealed in a museum case will get old and dull and dry and cracked with no one to oil it. They might sound like synonyms when you see them in real estate listings, but there's a distinct difference between "totally untouched" and "well maintained." This impenetrable house, it had been *well maintained*.

"And this title," she said, "it is German. It is *A Theory of Color and Palettes: My Struggle* by Adolf Hitler." She pulled it off the shelf and flicked to the copyright page. "First edition, published 1972. And it is autographed." She held up the book for me to see, but I was still looking at the kitchen down the hall. "Dedication," she read from the facing page, "to my dearest Geli, for staying by my side through our darkest hours."

The other thing that was bothering me was the kitchen at the end of that dark hall: it was bright, as though drenched in summer-morning sunshine. But when we left the bar it was almost dinnertime.

And this house had no power. There was no power on the entire block: someone had come through, felled the poles like trees, and scrapped the transformers for the copper.

But here in the crooked house you didn't need power to have light. I looked up at the lovely old cut-glass fixtures in the hall and sitting room. They were dark. Still, our little library was lit by an even, buttery glow. It was downright cozy.

Anja was paging through Hitler's theory of color, totally absorbed.

I thought about that word, *"absorbed."* I thought about how flies got stuck in slick, cozy pitcher plants, and then got absorbed. I craned around to look at the front door, which still stood open. The sun was low and fiery, resting on the Detroit skyline like a dying candle flame and casting all the shadows as long shards. Still, there was enough ambient light out there that you could have read a magazine standing out on the sidewalk. So why— or, more importantly, *how*—were the parlor windows so dark?

I finally let go of the perfect, polished banister and stepped into that terminally cozy sitting room, crossing to the windows. It was midnight-dark out there, a dark you never get in Detroit.

And there was no Detroit out beyond those windows, only distant, jagged mountains cutting into a sky choked with stars. I couldn't tell you if they were familiar stars or not. The light pollution is so bad in Metro Detroit that all you can ever see —even on the clearest night—is the moon and Orion and part of the Big Dipper.

But this, this was more stars than I'd seen in my entire life, total. Stars like fistful upon fistful of white sand scattered across a swath of black velvet.

I wanted to point this out to Anja, but as I slowly pivoted, my eyes slid over the big, cozy hearth. There was a pair of sneakers on the mantel, a pair of like-new LeBron 11s—the limited edition "What the LeBron?" ones, with their crazy black-light-blender-puke rainbow scribbles and splashes. Ugly, ugly fucking shoes. Still, those shoes are coveted by teens and corner boys alike. They wait in line for hours and then pay hundreds for them, or get them from resellers online for a grand. But there was something off about these shoes: the left sneaker had a weird brown tiger-stripe motif cutting through the hot pinks and glowing teals. I took a couple steps closer and wasn't shocked to see that the brown was old blood. There appeared to be a healthy portion of a foot still in that left shoe. The sock was neatly snipped off and singed, showing a little slice of dark skin. The exposed cut was blackened like a steak fresh off the grill. The neat end of the bone was glistening ivory sliced with laser precision. I sniffed the air without thinking, but it didn't smell like a cookout. I was grateful for that.

"I think we better go," I said.

"*Já*," Anja said, distracted, only half-listening. "But this book, these books are very interesting."

"Yeah," I said, "I hear that." I glanced over and saw her chewing her thumbnail distractedly as she read. Past her, in the front hall, I couldn't see the door—not from that angle—but I could see the light of the setting sun on the iridescent Pewabic tiles, slowly stretching and dimming. I turned back to the bay window, where it was still midnight in a galaxy far, far away. "There *is* a helluva view from this hilltop," I heard myself say. That window seat looked pretty damn comfy. I could sit there and really watch those stars, really get a good look at those jagged mountains. Maybe let my eyes adjust and see what was in the dim landscape between here and there.

Then there was a sound. A small sound in that silent house, like a door latching upstairs. A totally normal sound in an old, crooked house. But it was followed by an odd little clack and whine further back in the house, like an old-school camera flash charging. Anja and I were startled from our reveries. She didn't bother checking her camera because she already knew what I immediately saw: no flash on that bad boy. I suddenly remembered the shoes on the mantle and was shocked I'd somehow forgotten about them.

Our eyes locked. Anja looked desperate and lost, the way an orangutan in a concrete cage looks. It was plain on her face that I looked just the same.

"*Huldufólk*," she whispered.

"Hilde who?"

"We must go," she hissed.

Another shuffle and creak.

"Yeah," I replied.

There was a third shuffling step, maybe at the top of those stairs.

"And we must go quietly." Her voice quavered.

"Yeah." I offered her my hand. She reached out and took it, and we padded across the room like Hansel and Gretel getting the fuck out of the gingerbread house.

Back on the porch, I wanted to have one of those "Phew! Safe again!" shared moments, like in a movie. But it didn't *feel* safe again. It felt like we were standing in the gaping jaws of a lunging shark. It didn't feel safe again down on the front walk, either. Nor on the sidewalk.

Neither of us spoke as we walked back to the Old Miami. Anja had her arms wrapped around her chest, hugging Hitler's *Theory of Color*, her index finger still marking the place where she'd left off. I tried to explain to myself what had just happened, what we'd felt and what it meant. I didn't get anywhere with it. It was like trying to solve an equation that's nothing but variables; there was nowhere to start.

It wasn't a great first date. I wasn't shocked that

she didn't text me the next day—which I spent working on my brownstone's front staircase.

But try as I might, I couldn't slip into my carpentry groove. My mind kept wandering back to Fleis-chermann's crooked house, and whatever it was that quietly rambled its halls. And I kept thinking about Fleischermann himself, how he'd jumped right into that mystery door without hesitation, and how, despite not being his dad, he was still as hard as a mouthful of sixpenny nails, just the same.

I kept telling myself that, hard as he was, Fleischer-mann still couldn't get the place open; I had the only keys right there on my belt. But even nice enhanced-security Schlage SC4s with *DO NOT DUPLICATE* stamped on them are easy to copy. And hard men are somewhat notorious for a constitutional inability to let well enough alone.

Part of me wanted to call my dad—Dr. Washing-ton, still going strong despite advancing age —'cause old doctors know enough to know they don't know it all. Dad would believe me about the crooked house. And doctors, by their nature, go at problems with Occam's razor in hand. I badly needed someone to help me cut through the bullshit.

But I didn't make that call, because I knew that at the first break in the convo, Dad'd ask if I'd given my Architect Registration Exam another thought. It wasn't the question that I couldn't stand, it was the disappointment in his voice as he asked it, already knowing what my answer'd be.

Finally, I just drove out to Fleischermann's offices, even though I had the morning off. The "offices" of Fleischermann and Fleischermann Properties, Inc., are barely outside Detroit, a single unit in a shitty little strip mall with a decent address. Stepping in was always a blast from the past: threadbare brown industrial carpet, fake-walnut wallboard, dusty framed certificates and ancient concept drawings of retail centers the Original Butcher Man had conceived, built, leased, managed, sold, bought back, and torn down before I'd hit middle school.

The door chimed as I came in. Lennie was sitting on the swaybacked sofa parked next to the door, crammed between two beat-down Bankers Boxes full of papers. He stared fixedly into an iPad, little white earbuds screwed into his head, lips set in concentration. It was *Iron Man 3*, which meant I could look forward to Lennie's brief lecture on

Tony Stark—who, despite being America's favorite billionaire playboy philanthropist, is still only the fourth-richest fictional character, according to *Forbes* magazine's "2013 Forbes Fictional 15." Numero Uno is Scrooge McDuck, Glenn.

"Can you give me a ride to my parents' house?" Lennie yelled to be heard over the superhero antics blasting through his earbuds.

I told him, "Yeah," and he screwed up his face quizzically, so I shouted it louder.

"Who's that?" Fleischermann yelled through his half-open office door. "Leonard, who's here?"

"It's me," I said, crossing the reception area—which was hardly three strides wide, including the detour around a wobbly card table buried in stratified layers of blueprints and site plans.

"Good," he said as I stepped into his doorway, "'cause—"

"Because we gotta talk about that crooked house."

Fleischermann waved the topic off without rising or looking up from the little yellow pad of paper he was writing on. "That shit," he said, "is SEP."

S.E.P.: "Somebody Else's Problem."

"You flipped it?" I asked.

"Yeah," he said, still not looking up. "More or less. Here." He tore the top page from the yellow tablet and handed it across to me.

"What's this?" I glanced down. There were seven addresses, three on one street, three on another, and one by itself. I only recognized one street name and couldn't place it, but guessed we were dealing with a block of houses, all on adjacent lots.

"I need you to check those out, gimme an idea of what it'll take to clear the parcel."

"Yeah, OK. But the crooked house, how the hell did you flip that? When'd you even list it?"

"Didn't need to; buyer came looking."

My stomach sank. "A buyer popped up out of the blue for that specific lot?" I asked, incredulous.

Fleischermann was feigning interest in something on his laptop. "Hmm?" He frowned in faux concentration.

"It was Officers Jones and Washington!" Lennie

called from the reception sofa, yelling to be heard over the crash-and-boom only he could hear.

I fumed. "Where the fuck did those cops get a hundred and thirty-seven grand?" I asked Fleischermann.

He continued to pretend to be engrossed in his laptop. I stood there, sharply flicking the corner of the sheet of paper, making it crack like a tiny snare drum. Finally Fleischermann rolled his eyes, then switched gears and brightened his demeanor. He snapped the laptop shut and came around his desk.

"Dick Schnabel," he said, fixing me with a broad salesman's grin, "financed it. It's Dick's deal. Getting his Moon rock back, or the next-best thing. The cops just run his errands so he doesn't have to drive way the fuck down here from the Land of Milk, Honey, and Three-Acre Manicured Lawns."

"Dick Schnabel. He's a serious dude, I'm told."

"That he is."

"And he paid cash money for a house no one can go in?"

"Something like that." I caught him looking at the little sheet of yellow paper in my hand.

"Oh, dag!" I groaned, frustrated with Fleischermann. "He *didn't* pay cash money?"

"Those properties," Fleischermann insisted, pointing at the yellow slip, "are *better* than cash money!"

I looked at the addresses again. As before, only one street name jumped out at me, *Trinity Ave*. It clicked into place like lock and key.

"These are in *Brightmoor*?" The Brightmoor neighborhood, in the northwest corner of the city: largely derelict, mostly known as a dump for old appliances, bald tires, and dead bodies. Last I'd checked, the median home value out there was something like ten grand—and that was for *occupiable* units.

"There's a project going into Brightmoor," Fleischermann said, "some sort of interagency state-federal-international public-private partnership thing with Homeland Security and INS and Canada."

"That's a lot of hyphens," I said.

He went on as though he hadn't heard my snark. "We clear it and grade it now—and I can get the city to pay us to do that, I bet." Fleischermann was smiling but his forehead was beaded with flop sweat. *He* was trying to sell *me* on the idea. It was pitiful. "Then the interagency-whoevers will pay an easy half-mil for the development-ready land. It's double money for nothing, practically."

"And so you and Dick Schnabel did a swap?"

He shrugged. "Swap plus cash." The breezy way he added those last two words made it pretty clear that Fleischermann was not the one receiving the cash.

My God. Poor old Butcher Man, Jr., hadn't just bought the useless house, he'd then gone and traded it for a fistful of magic beans and paid for the privilege. I pasted a smile on my face and nodded, feigning admiration.

Fleischermann slapped me on the back. "Good. Good! You and Lennie go out there Monday, make an estimate on what it'll take to clear it and fence it." We stepped out into the reception area. "Can you give Lennie a lift to his folks'?" He didn't bother waiting for my answer before continuing:

"Good. Oh, hey, whatever happened to the keys to the place, the crooked house? You still got 'em?"

That shiny Schlage and bent-wafer key were nestled in the janitor's knot clipped to my belt. "Naw." I said, "I gave them to Lennie to give to you." I tapped Lennie on the shoulder to get his attention—he couldn't hear a thing with *Iron Man 3* screaming in his ears—then gestured at the door. Lennie nodded and pulled his earbuds, carefully wrapping them around the iPad before setting it on the vacant receptionist's desk. "That was your only set of keys?"

"Yeah." Fleischermann shrugged, turning back to his office, totally unperturbed, which was totally unlike him. He scooped up his phone, settled back into his chair, and started dialing. "Forget it," he said. "S.E.P. Cops didn't even ask." He chuckled. "Fucking DPD probably already had a set. Those fuckers are crooked as a dog's leg, amiright?" Whoever he was calling picked up and Fleischermann's attention snapped away from us. "Myra? Myra, Felix Fleischermann. Yep." He laughed. "The Butcher Man himself. Listen, can you put Gil on?"

Lennie and I headed out into the parking lot.

"He means the back leg," Lennie said as we crossed the asphalt.

"I know."

"Because a dog's front legs are really straight."

"I know." I unlocked the passenger door and continued around the truck. My phone was ringing. I dug it out of my pocket, still standing in the autumn sunshine, one hand on the frame of the S-10's open door. It was a Detroit number, but not one I recognized.

"This Glenn Washington?" A female voice, hard and black, ready to brook no bullshit. I sighed, assuming it was a Fleischermann tenant with some little five-alarm pain in the ass to derail my day.

"Yes," I said politely.

"Why the hell you take Anja around to a bunch of blighted shit?" the woman snapped. "Don't you know she's from *Iceland*? Don't you listen to NPR? About Iceland's economy and shit? You know those people don't have a goddamn ounce of sense!"

Bewildered, I got about three words into asking who the fuck I was talking to when she cut me off.

"I'm her roommate, dumbass. Anja texted me your number last night, and this morning she went back to take some more pictures, and now she's got cop problems and she's not answering her phone. So maybe you hustle your black ass down wherever you took her to last night and smooth that shit out, Mr. Man?"

I instantly recognized this brand of Detroit belligerence for what it was: the thorny blanket you pulled up over your head to hide how anxious you were.

"Yeah, OK, let's wind that sass back." I slid into the truck and cranked the engine. "I get that you are unhappy with the current situation."

"Also," Lennie piped up, "you can't make a dog's back leg straight. That's why you say someone is crooked as a dog leg, 'cause part of the point is that you can't make them straight. That's just how they are, and you have to live with it."

I waved for Lennie to shut the fuck up. "I'm on my way to straighten out this crooked shit as we speak," I said into the phone. "This is not a big deal. I totally know what's happened and it's just some standard-issue Napoleonic cop bullshit."

"Mmmm-hm," she said, not sounding impressed. Then I heard her take a breath to resume tearing into me and hung up. I dropped the phone into the cup holder. It immediately started ringing.

"Phone's ringing," Lennie announced.

I put it on vibrate and let it rattle around with my loose change as I explained to Lennie about the Old Miami and Anja and going in the house and the things we heard moving around in there—all of which Lennie accepted with equanimity. That's the nice thing about chilling with a learning-disabled dude: he's totally acclimated to things being amazing and unintelligible. Lennie didn't know how the crooked house worked, but he also didn't understand how the iPad worked or how lockpicking worked or why the Hershey's Kisses were called "kisses" when they looked like garden gnome hats. The crooked house did not in any way upset the balance of the world for Lennie because Lennie was not at all deluded that he understood the world to begin with.

There was a police cruiser angled to the curb in front of the crooked house. The gate was open and Cop A was up on the porch messing with the door while Cop B hung back next to the car. Anja sat on the curb, arms wrapped around her knees.

Cop B glanced up as we crunched around the corner. "Look at that," he called to Cop A. "It's Washington, Glenn, no priors, no warrants, no outstanding tickets, no middle name." My stomach ice-knotted. There was no way in hell that cop should have remembered me; they deal with dozens of penny-ante assholes like me every day. The fact that I'd lodged in his head boded poorly.

Cop A shook his head as he sauntered down the steps, tossing and catching a big knot of keys in one hand. "Figures." He paused to latch the gate and engage the combination lock. "I wonder if he knows Einarsdóttir, Anja Kvaran, no priors, no warrants, no outstanding tickets, no current student visa."

Anja hung her head lower, letting her bangs shield her eyes.

"We've met," I said flatly.

"Figures," he repeated.

"House locked up?" Cop B asked his partner. He

kept his eyes glued to his citation pad, his voice carefully over-casual.

"Still locked," Cop A said. He stopped tossing his knot and held it aloft by a single worn key, an enhanced-security reverse Schlage SC4. "Reminds me: were you ever able to get in that day your boss sent you out here, Mr. Washington?" His eyes were hard and cold and exploratory, like a bad doctor's fingers. Trying to feel out what I knew, who I'd told, who I might tell.

"Nope," I said honestly, "me and Lennie couldn't get in that day."

"Hunh. I know those 'enhanced security' Schlages are a bitch, but I'd'a thought a big bad bonded ALA-certified intermediate locksmith like you could git 'er done. You *sure* you couldn't get that door open?"

"Couldn't get in," I repeated flatly.

He nodded. "Damn shame your boss never found his keys."

I gritted my teeth. I am not a great liar.

Then Cop A cocked his head, as though he'd just had a really swell idea. "You know, seeing as how you bold explorers are so curious about this property, maybe I ought to open it up and let you in for a look-see." He jiggled the keys, as though he was trying to lure a cat out from under the sofa. "Let you satisfy your curiosity about this old house." It was stated as an offer, but clearly meant as a threat.

Anja had started quietly crying.

Cop B stopped writing, instead watching his partner warily. "What are you doing?" He gave every word equal weight.

"It's cool," I said. "Officer. Our boss sold the property. It's SEP now."

"*SEP?*" Cop A asked.

"*Somebody Else's Problem.* Sir. We won't be giving this parcel a second thought."

Cop A smiled at this, smiled honestly. "I'm glad we have an understanding."

Cop B kept his face passive. He slowly ripped the ticket from his pad.

"I'm issuing Ms. Einarsdóttir a summons for second-degree trespassing." He said this professionally, to no one in particular. "It's my determination that, as a foreign national with limited English, she was unable to ascertain that this was private property."

Cop A, his eyes still locked on mine, helpfully tapped the NO TRESPASSING sign that I myself had zip-tied to the gate.

"That will likely carry a fine," Cop B continued. "Trespassing in the *first* degree—*intentional* trespassing—carries a fine *and* up to one year in Wayne County Correctional." Anja was still immobile on the curb, shoulders bunched together, knees drawn up, head down. When Cop B held out the summons, she took it without looking up. "New property holders are very eager to prosecute trespassers," he said evenly. "This ain't a playground, kids."

Cop A waggled his keys at us scoldingly. "You li'l rascals stay out of trouble, now," he admonished, "and we'll see you in court, Ms. Einarsdóttir."

She nodded, her bangs jigging.

They climbed into their car. Cop A tapped the glass, then gave me a little "toodle-oo" wave before pulling off.

"Hunh," Lennie said, hands on hips, "Officers Jones and Washington didn't even say 'Hello.'"

"They're busy, Len. They're on the clock."

"Still, Wheaton's Law, Glenn."

"*Wheaton's Law*," I agreed. *Don't be a dick.*

He turned to Anja. "Are you going to need a lawyer? Because my brother-in-law is almost a partner at Hockman, Bluestein, Burnham, and Brown, Attorneys-at-Law."

"There is a man locked in the house," Anja whispered. "I have locked a man in the house unintentionally."

It hit me like a punch in the nose: the night before, when Anja and I fled, I never checked to be sure the door locked behind us. I wasn't even sure I'd *closed* it.

Anja didn't look up as she spoke. "I stayed awake late in the night," she said, "reading Adolf Hitler's *Theory of Color*. My German is not lovely, and the book was very tedious. Yet also . . ." She squinted, scrutinizing the summons without seeing it. "Yet also fascinating. Slowly it dawned upon me that the book was . . . Enchanted?" She looked up at me, her bangs falling away from her eyes. "Charmed? Be-witch-éd? *Já?*"

I thought about the landscape beyond the sitting room's bay window, and about that extra-comfy window seat. I thought about how easy just looking at that comfy bench had made it to forget about the severed foot on the mantel.

"*Já,*" I said, "charmed."

"And with that I understood how grave was my mistake in taking the book from the *Huldufólk* which dwell within the crooked house."

"That means *bad elves*, Glenn," Lennie stage-whispered. "I saw a documentary on YouTube called *Investigation into the Invisible World:* Huldufólk *of Iceland—Elves, Ghosts, Sea Monsters, or Extraterrestrials?*" Lennie said the punctuation as words: "colon," "dash," "question mark."

Anja had gone back to scrutinizing that stupid summons, but was otherwise empty-handed. No camera, no book. Her shoulder bag was a little thing; no room for that heavy hardcover.

"You put the book back?"

"*Já,*" she said, "I returned to the house this morning

and the door stood open. Just a crack. I came in, and it was like coming in to a warm library from out of a blizzard." She spoke steadily, without inflection. "But when the book was replaced up on the shelf, I did not feel . . . free. I felt just as tempted by each book."

One in particular had caught her eye—she couldn't recall what it looked like, if it was worn or new, leatherbound or a paperback galley—but she remembered the title vividly: *Implications and Applications of Wheaton's Law: Fluid Dynamics in N!-Dimensional Rotations (third illustrated edition)* by Dr. Anja Kvaran Einarsdóttir, PhD. It was then that she discovered that she was already hearing the camera-flash-charging sound, and had been hearing it since she entered the house.

"With the sound," she said, lips quivering, "I felt a shadow cast over me, but also inside me. The shadow was like a net that surrounded me from within, but also like a fishhook that pulled me down into myself. It was dreadful. But it was also dreadfully . . . easy. Dreadfully easy to take another book from the shelf, to look at a few more pages. To relax in the place, even as the shadow net closed, dragging me into myself, through myself to some bad other place."

She was shaking now, her voice quavering as she spoke. "I relaxed. I began to consider which book to next select. It dawned on me that I had been considering for a very long time, and that I was no longer considering but just simply standing, and that there was something wrong with . . . not only with my brains, but with my body. I could feel my body twisting tight, like a rag being wrung out. My mouth gaped, stiff, full of the taste of gunpowder and old meat. It was . . ." Her lips twisted and she shook her head involuntarily, like a dog trying to clear a snootful of pepper spray. "It was awful. I gagged and tore myself loose from . . . from this deformed state. Tore myself loose from myself. I turned to run and ran straight into the frame of the door. And this, this I believe saved me. I was thwacked between the eyes so hard, the hurt shocked me awake. I stumbled out of the parlor and glanced back toward the kitchen, and there in the doorway was an awful living darkness. It was the hidden folk who dwell there. I flew from the house and slammed the door behind me. But . . ." She chewed her lips and I saw, unbelievably, that she was blushing. "But when I heard the latch click, I was in an instant overwhelmed by this tremendous loss, heartbroken to have given up the opportunity to sink into the dreadful delight of all of those tedious, boring books. I turned, I grabbed the knob, twisting it with regret. But it was locked. And it was then that I saw the monster stumble through the doorway, into clearer light."

She sniffled mightily and finally looked at us. Her eyes burned with a weird defiant regret. "It was no monster, no bad faerie: it was a bald man in a gray chalk-stripe business suit. He, too, was fascinated by the crooked house. But watchful, like a cat scenting something that might be dinner, or might be keen on making dinner of him. I banged on the window and his head twitched, as one might at the bump in the night. This cost him dearly. Whatever he had been watching for, it took that moment to spring. It jerked the man once, hard, like a poor puppeteer abusing a hateful marionette. The man stumbled back into the dining room, and he was gone." She paused, and then admitted, "But not gone. I could see his struggles in the shadows for a long, long time."

She was crying now in earnest.

"And then the officers were there, shouting to get

the fuck from that door, to not touch that fucking door. Hands were on my wrists, like iron straps." Her shoulders shook but her voice stayed even now. "The officer with the glasses—" she meant Cop A "—he dragged me from the porch and asked many question which I could not follow. And," she sniffed, "and also questions I pretended to not follow, questions about the things within the house."

I looked at Lennie, who was twitching his mouth like a worried bunny. "There's bad elves in the house?" he asked.

"I doubt that."

Anja looked up, eyes blazing. "I can hear you, you know? You are not speaking secret codes."

I held up my hands placatingly. "You're right: we're being dicks. Wheaton's Law. I apologize."

She sniffled, scrunching her nose and pursing her mouth like a kitten about to sneeze.

I clapped my hands and pasted a big fake smile on my face. "Let's go to Greek Town! You been to Greek Town?" She shook her head, confused. "You'll love it!" I said. "White people *love* Greek

Town! We'll order a *saganaki*, get Lennie's bro-by-law on the phone, and start straightening out this summons. I bet those jokers aren't even planning to show up for your court date, so it'll be thrown out anyway."

She stitched her brow and I turned my smile up twenty watts. "'*Saganaki*,'" I said with air quotes, "is that Greek cheese they set on fire while yelling, 'Opa!' Then they put the fire out with lemon wedges. You'll love it."

"*Já*, I have eaten the *saganaki* cheese, Glenn. Greeks and Chinese open restaurants wherever they settle. You are suggesting we leave?"

"*Já.*" I flinched; her stupid accent was infecting me. "Yeah, I am. Specifically, I'm suggesting we leave well enough alone."

She was incredulous. "There is a man in the house, Glenn. Trapped in the house. You have keys to the house. I know this is true."

"We should let him out of the house, is what she's saying," Lennie added.

I clenched my teeth. "Yeah, I got that, Len. But I'm maybe feeling like we should cease fucking with this house. Like, just to be clear, let us all recall that Cop A—"

"Officer Jones, Glenn—"

"That Officer Jones was *threatening* us with the house; people do not classically threaten people with not-dangerous shit. Like, in contrast, I *offered* to buy everyone *saganaki.*"

The look Anja gave me after I said that, I don't think we have a word for that look in English. I'm sure they do in German, and it's thirty-eight letters long, and it translates to *"The manner in which you look upon a man who has, in his highly predictable cowardice, not quite risen to the level of being worthy of your contempt."*

"Fine!" I spat. "Dumbasses." I hauled myself over the fence and stomped up the walk. The chain link rattled behind me as Lennie and Anja followed suit. I clomped up the steps and into the shadow of the recessed entry, slid the key into the knob before I could loose my nerve, turned the lock, and threw the door open.

I'd intended to holler, *"Ollie-ollie-ox-in-free!"* and wait for whoever to come out—'cause while I *am* a coward, I'm still not an idiot.

But then I saw Anja's man, and I couldn't say a word. He was back past the parlor, just inside the dim dining room. He stood on one foot, bent forward with his right hand clamped to his gut, like he had cramps. His body was tense, vibrating with effort, and his free arm out, bracing him against the wall. But there was no wall there. And he had only one leg. No gore—the missing leg hadn't been torn off. No dangling pant-leg, either. He was just a one-legged dude in a one-legged suit, natural as could be. Insanely, I wondered why Anja hadn't said the dude was one-legged. It was sort of a major detail to gloss over.

But none of that was what froze the words in my mouth.

There was a *thing* in the room with the man.

There was a thing in the room, and I couldn't figure out what the hell it was. At first I took it to be a shadow, but that wasn't right. Shadows are flat, cast onto a surface, and this darkness hung in the air. And it was grappling with the man. The thing moved in jagged fits, like a time-lapse film of germination, or video that's dropping frames. It elongated and contracted, bulging like motor oil floating in zero Gs, extending and withdrawing appendages of some sort—arms, maybe? Or roots? Or tentacles? One of these extrusions was a broad, flat wing. Another was spiky, infinitely, infinitesimally branching like a fractal.

Limbs, at any rate. It sprouted and absorbed these limbs, which caressed the horrified businessman, pulling him like taffy.

And I didn't particularly care, for some reason. It was, literally, *fascinating*, in the absolute oldest sense of that word. The house was overflowing with that high-pitched, ever-rising camera-charging whine, so full that it rattled your guts and buzzed the fluid in your eyes. The sound made it hard to think, and also made it hard to care about the fact that it was hard to think.

The limbfull shadow-thing was black, but that black had color in it, the way there's color in the blackness behind your closed eyes. And it had textures, like concrete or tree bark or gloppy crude oil washed up on a beach. And in that texture there was a glittering. It dawned on me that maybe that glitter wasn't glitter, but distant lights. Or stars. Maybe the shadow-thing wasn't a form taking up space at all, but a hole you'd drop through, falling for years without touching bottom.

I could hear the man's little jibbering grunts, and the hard leather sole of his single-tassel loafer gritting against the broad boards. But the thing he was tangling with made no sound—and why would it? Do shadows make sounds? Do holes?

But damned if that crippled dude in the suit wasn't trying to wrestle the thing down.

"That's Dick Schnabel!" Lennie gasped in my ear, pushing into the house. I didn't think to grab him. "Mr. Schnabel!" Lennie shouted, tromping past the sitting room. "Jeez! Are you OK?"

The man—Dick Schnabel—was startled by Lennie's braying voice, and so was the air-shadow thing; it released Schnabel and slithered away, origami-folding itself up into thin air.

Dick Schnabel unfolded as the thing retreated. His missing leg unwound from nowhere at all, revealing a shoeless foot in a gold-toed men's dress sock.

He bent forward, left hand planted on his thigh, chest heaving as though he'd just sprinted up six flights of stairs. Lennie set one of his big mitts on the man's shoulder, again asking if Mr. Schnabel was OK.

I crossed the threshold into the house without a second thought, but froze just past the sitting room. The man's right hand, the one pressed to his gut, wasn't a hand at all, it was a mashed knot of flesh like a crumpled ball of paper—and I mean *exactly* like a wad of paper: sharp creases, pointed angles, no blood. Then that unfolded, too, just like the leg. Again, no gore or goo or glistening, no broken fingers, just a standard-issue hand.

Holding a gun.

Dick Schnabel's index finger rested straight across the trigger guard, as is the habit of folks accustomed to holding guns. The pistol itself was one I only knew from playing combat video games: an FN Five-SeveN, pricy and no-nonsense, optimized for converting living mutherfuckers to dead mutherfuckers with all due celerity. A serious gun.

This was the notorious Dick Schnabel. I understood, deep to my bones, what Lennie had meant: this was a serious, serious dude.

You could hear a pin drop in the crooked house; the high-pitched squeal had left with the awful ever-folding shadowtree.

"My watch says I've been in here two days," the man with the gun told no one in particular.

Two days. He'd been in here when I'd shown the place to Anja. I looked at his shoeless foot and thought again about what we'd heard, especially the dragging step. The front door latched shut, and I looked back to see Anja standing uncertainly near the broad archway that opened into the sitting room.

"Two days," Schnabel repeated, "but I've seen the sun rise eight times out these windows—" he gestured vaguely with the gun, indicating that he meant all of the windows in the house "—and I've seen it set twenty-two."

I dug out my cell phone to check the time. Schnabel chuckled ruefully, and when I glanced down I saw why: no service, no time, just zeros.

"No reception in here," Schnabel said, holding up his free hand to show me the old-fashioned watch on his wrist. "An automatic. Self-winding. Bastard keeps ticking as long as I do. Upstairs, under the eaves, there's a spot with dormer windows opposite each other. I saw the sun rise and set in that room simultaneously." His voice was soft and dull as he puzzled over what he'd encountered sojourning the house. "The funny thing was, if you looked out the sunset window, if you really really looked, off in the distance you could see another house. And, I swear to fucking God, if you timed it right and squinted, you could see a little fucker way up in the attic, facing away." Dick Schnabel's eyes sharpened as he looked at me. "Don't gotta tell you that guy was wearing my suit, do I? And had my bald spot? And raised his hand when I raised mine?"

"You must be hungry," Lennie said, "if you've been in here two days."

Schnabel nodded, still distracted, a serious dude with a lot on his mind. Anja stepped closer, digging in her purse, and handed him a LUNA Bar. Schnabel looked at the label: *The whole nutrition bar for women.*

"Great," he scoffed, "now I'm gonna grow a vagina."

"*Já,*" she deadpanned, "an entire garden of vaginas. You will sell them in bunches at Eastern Market. Unclefucker."

Gotta say, I have enormous respect for a woman

who will straight-up call an armed man "uncle-fucker" to his face.

Schnabel smiled, patronizingly pleased with this feistiness. "Thanks, sweetie," he said, peeling the wrapper off the bar using the thumb and index finger of his right hand while still gripping the little pistol with the other three fingers.

"I really think we oughta go, Mr. Schnabel," Lennie said gently, leading Schnabel out of the gloomy dining room. "I think you hurt your foot." I looked down at Schnabel's stocking-clad foot, and there was indeed something badly wrong with his leg. It seemed to bear weight OK, but the calf was misshapen and jagged, like something from a Futurist sculpture or Cubist painting. Not one of the blurry-motion ones, like Marcel Duchamp's "Nude Descending a Staircase" or Giacomo Balla's "Dynamism of a Dog on a Leash." More like that Umberto Boccioni sculpture "Unique Forms of Continuity in Space." Just Google it later and you'll see.

Schnabel's pant-leg was partially inside out, pulled through itself, like a tailor had tried to make Klein-bottle trousers. But that impossibly inside-out section of pant-leg? It was pulled through his sock and leg, too. Once again, no blood or gore, just some bad geometry, like a 3-D rendering done on shitty software.

"Doesn't that hurt?" I asked, wondering how surgeons were going to separate his pants from his leg—wondering how his foot was still attached at all.

"Lotta shit hurts," he said, "doesn't matter—" And then something in his bearing changed, like a cat glimpsing a caterpillar. Schnabel looked at Lennie, and then me, then back to Lennie, then addressed us both: "Jesus. You're those two idiots that work for Fleischermann, whatsis . . ." Schnabel snapped his fingers to jog his memory. "Epstein and . . ." He snapped again. "And . . . black guy."

"We're not idiots!" Lennie huffed. I just sighed.

Schnabel cocked an eyebrow in mock incredulity, then gave me a second look. "Yeah," he said, "OK. You're not *both* idiots." Now he was just talking to me. "But you both work for Fleischermann, doing his crooked little shit. And Fleischermann *is* a fucking idiot." His eyes crawled into me, rifling through the folds of my brain, unerringly taking my measure.

"You seem to be feeling pretty crummy," Lennie reiterated, leading Schnabel by the elbow, "and Glenn's friend Anja says this house might have bad elves." Anja nodded. "We should leave."

"Leave." He chuckled. "I've been trying to leave since I realized Washington and Jones had locked me in. Hey—" he looked past Anja "—is that the front door?"

We all turned to look at the door. I was unsurprised to see that the knob was keyed on the inside, too, with no thumb-bolt or latch. Folks used to do that. I think it's illegal now, to have doors with keyed locks inside and out. Fire codes and shit.

Anja looked back to Schnabel. "*Já.* It is the door."

"I've been trying to find the fucking front door for the last thirty hours. Is it unlocked?" he asked eagerly.

"Probably not," I said. "It latches when it's closed. But it doesn't matter. I've got the keys."

Schnabel looked at the brass key still pinched between my index finger and thumb. "Fleischermann said the spares were lost."

I didn't know what to say, and so I said nothing. This pleased Schnabel, who read into it whatever suited him.

"I know what a dipshit like Fleischermann can afford. You're selling yourself below market," Schnabel told me. "Lucky for you, I'm hiring. And I pay premium rates for top performers. I've currently got a pair of shitty employees I need to terminate. Today. Let's consider this your interview."

I didn't know what to say about that, either. I'm going to level with you: he was right that being Fleischermann's lawn boy was beneath me. Still, I wasn't sure that I wanted to be whatever Officers Jones and Washington were to this serious dude.

I stepped past everyone, slid the key into the knob lock, turned it, and was reassured when the door pulled in and swung to lay flush against the wall that shielded the hearth from any front-door draft. If I'd only had the view through the parlor windows to go by, I'd have assumed it was dead of night. But autumn sunshine poured in the open front door. It was still just lunchtime in Detroit. Somewhere, far back in the house, there was that camera-flash *clack*. For the first time since he'd come back to himself a few minutes earlier, Schnabel was visibly rattled.

"Chop-chop, kids," he whispered, shooing with his gun hand, his finger still meticulously across the trigger guard. "Times a-wastin'."

I stepped through the door and stumbled into the night-dim kitchen. Same Hoosier cabinet, same icebox, same ancient lino floor. Through the little windows over the deep double kitchen sink, I saw a big sliver of blood moon sinking below the distant mountains. Down the hall, at the front door, Schnabel was still shooing Lennie and Anja out into the sun-drenched yard. Lennie stepped through the doorway.

And piled into me from behind. "Fuck." I sighed. Anja—still down the hall by the front door—turned around and our eyes locked. She looked absolutely hopeless. Schnabel stood at the threshold, staring out.

"Where the fuck did those *farkakte klotzen* go?" Schnabel asked the bright noon air. Then he stepped out.

I heard his distinctive gait on the linoleum: the click of one hard-soled tassel loafer, the shuffle of a stocking-clad foot. "Well, ain't that fucking predictable?" he told the kitchen.

Lennie was looking around the room. "Hunh," he said, the sort of mildly curious grunt a *Jeopardy!* viewer uses when Alex Trebek reveals that, "This nine-letter word for an unfoldable hypercube starts and ends with *T*."

Anja was already walking back to join us—taking the scenic route through the house. There was a stiff breeze outside—I could see it blowing around a plastic grocery sack—but not a lick of air came in the front door, underscoring how stale it was there inside the crooked house, like being sealed in a museum case.

"So, the keys do not trump the house, *já*?" she said as she joined us in the kitchen. "Maybe the officers shall return and let us out?"

"Fat fuckin' chance," Schnabel said. "This is their goddamn roach motel."

"Roach motels have this sticky goo on the floor to keep the roach in," Lennie volunteered. "These floors are clean. This is more like a lobster trap."

"They call 'em lobster pots," Schnabel said, nettled.

Lennie went on as though no one had spoken. Trying to stop a Lenniesplanation was as hopeless as scolding an avalanche.

"They're like a wood cage with a funnel entrance at one end. Lobsters can come in easy, but then they can't come back out again. This is more like that, since lobster traps make it real easy to go one way and real hard to go the other. Like here. Also, lobster traps have 'rooms' in them, and one room is called a 'kitchen'—with the bait—while the other room is called a 'parlor,' where the lobsters hang out and wait for the lobsterman. This house also has several rooms, including a kitchen. And a parlor."

The cozy parlor, where you hang out waiting for the lobsterman from beyond the stars, reading books, looking through the windows, absent-minded and content. My guts went to water.

"Yeah, it's the Chinese Finger Trap of the Gods," Schnabel said, "but I think my fucking analogy stands: problems check in, and they don't check out. I hired Officers Turncoat and McBackstabby to exterminate problems without a trace. This is evidently how they did so. Ancient cop secret. For all I know, DPD has been shoving inconvenient troublemakers in here since Prohibition."

It was easy to imagine: you've got some scumbag that you can't make charges stick to, so you have someone lure him into the house—"Hey, Johnny, I heard there's a load of Canadian whiskey stashed in the basement of this crooked old house. I hear there's a couple keys of blow stashed in the basement of this crooked old house. We got a little girl tied up and passed out in the basement of this crooked old house."

Whatever. Slam the door and let Anja's bad elves take care of it.

'Course, it was also easy to imagine the mission creep. Starts out being a hush-hush thing used only on very exceptionally bad dudes. But convenience corrupts, and sooner than later I could see it becoming, "Hey, Johnny, that grand Mr. No-Name owes you? It's stashed down in the basement of this crooked old house. You wanna blow the whistle on some corrupt bullshit? Ain't safe to talk here, but I know this crooked old house . . ."

And so on.

Problems go in, and they don't come out.

"But they had a problem of their own?" I said—not really asking, just goading Schnabel. Most guys have a "Lenniesplaining" mode and Schnabel was no exception.

The serious dude smiled. "Yep. Turns out they didn't own their little Problem Solver. No one did: it was an abandoned property with a fucked-up title, and they just happened to wind up with the keys. That was their bind: at any time, their magic house could pop up on some list of blighted properties slated for demolition, and someone would actually come out and look at it. Which is exactly what *did* happen, invisible hand of the free fucking market and all that. When they came across you dumbasses fucking with it legit, they saw how they could own their little slice of heaven—if they found some putz to play straw man and finance it."

"And you're that putz."

Schnabel winced but he didn't argue. "It was fucking Fleischermann that fucked me." He sighed. "He didn't do it on purpose—because the fact is that he's a fucking *freier* by birth, a tool of the first degree. It was those fucking cops. The cops told me Fleischermann had come into an 'interesting' property—no details—and I gave him a call. When he told me about your little frontdoor-backdoor shenanigans, I was hooked. Did the paperwork sight unseen—and Jones and Washington were such dears, they took care of all the errand-boy shit, even gave me a lift down here so I wouldn't have to chance my suspension on that fucked-up road." He chuffed, shaking his head at his own folly. "Played right into their hands. Practically begged the cops to give me the grand tour. And that was it. I'll disappear without a trace, but the owner of the house—Schnabel Asset Group IV, LLC—will live on forever, paying taxes like clockwork. It'll be a hundred years before some intern gets down to sorting out why my fucking estate's got this one pissant property out in the fabulous ruins of BFE." He shook his head. "Fucking cops. Anyone who thinks cops are dumb is a fucking idiot."

"Do Officers Jones and Washington know about the bad elves?" Lennie asked, not looking at me or Schnabel, but instead staring past Anja's shoulder, toward the front door.

"Doubt it. I don't think they've ever set foot in here. Jones—" he meant Cop A "—wouldn't cross the threshold—held the door open for me like a doorman. Not that I noticed at the time. Shame on me for being overeager."

"Can the bad elves get out of the house?" Lennie whispered.

Schnabel turned to Lennie, annoyed. "How the hell would I know? As far as I can tell, *nothing* can get out of the house. You can't even shoot out the windows; bullets splatter like you're shooting at a steel block."

Lennie kept staring past Anja's shoulder, so I looked. The silent shadowtree-thing had descended the staircase. It wove and juddered toward the door on its long, angular limbs, then paused in the autumn sunshine, peering out the open door into the bright afternoon. I thought of Duchamp's "Nude Descending a Staircase," and again of that Boccioni sculpture, "Unique Forms of Continuity in Space." Maybe those guys had taken their own trip into a crooked house. Maybe somewhere on that tidy parlor bookshelf there was a slim academic monograph with a title like *Unique Forms of Continuity in Space: The Impact of Hyperdimensional Contact on Futurism, Dada, and 20th-Century Expression: Duchamp, Boccioni, Balla, and the*

Terrible Shadowtree from Beyond the Veil of Dead Stars by Glenn Washington, PhD.

Schnabel had fallen silent, his mouth a gray dash fading into the blue stubble of his cheeks. He glanced from me to Lennie, then turned to look at the front door himself. Anja stayed perfectly still, back toward the door and face stony.

"I will prefer," she whispered, "not to look."

Schnabel raised the pistol, pointing it toward Anja. She set her mouth but didn't flinch, didn't even blink. Lennie sucked in air.

But Schnabel wasn't aiming at her. He was aiming past her, aiming at the bad elf.

"Maybe let's not," I hissed.

"That thing," he said quietly, "has come to fuck us up. There's only two things that can happen now: either it goes *through* the door out into the wide, wide world and becomes Detroit's problem, or it *tries* to go through the door and pops in here with us."

"OK," I said, "but if you miss, or if the bullet passes through the elf, it's going to hit us."

At the front door, the angular hardwood shadow continued to jaggedly ooze and shimmer as it scoped out the view. It didn't appear to be aware of us way back in the kitchen.

"Maybe let us quietly go upstairs, *já?*" Anja indicated a narrow staircase that climbed up from an alcove alongside the pantry, almost lost in the shadow of the open back door.

"*Já,*" I agreed. Lennie let out a long, slow breath and nodded. It was a majority. Schnabel didn't nod his assent but he lowered the pistol. We silently climbed the steps—and, predictably, wound up in the basement. There was a moment halfway up when the stairway . . . flipped. Not *physically*, it didn't flip over like a canoe, but . . . *perspectively*? It was like being in an M. C. Escher litho: suddenly the upstairs were downstairs and we were stumbling out into the cellar's sourceless bare-bulb light.

It was a classic Detroit basement: damp and musty, with a pounded dirt floor. The walls were the foundation itself, made of cobblestones mortared in place with concrete.

Lennie coughed once, hard, then spat on the dirt floor.

"That's like riding the salt 'n' pepper shakers at the State Fair." He groaned, hand on his gut.

I nodded, my own stomach taking a single nauseated flop.

"You get used to it," Schnabel said absently, appraising the room. "This isn't how I got down here before. Last time I ducked into the upstairs coat closet and came out . . ." He looked around, frowning. "There," he said, nodding at a closed door. "It's a toolroom."

"Tools?" I asked, although I didn't really have any plan. Dig our way to freedom? It sorta seemed like the only option, if no doors were going to cooperate. But then I imagined the curve balls we might get thrown when we exited the house's envelope that way. I shuddered. Would we drop into open space, only to crack back down on the pitched slate roof? Or something worse?

"Yeah, there's tools," he said, "but it might as well be a fucking display at the Henry Ford: it's brace-and-bits and mauls and the big saws they hang on the walls of bars up north."

I discovered I was hearing that sound again, like the cycling up of a camera flash. It was directly above us. I looked up. No ceiling or subflooring, just the undersides of the broad floorboards. There were long, hairline splinters of light where the boards met. We could see the shifting darkness of the shadow being, casting left to right, sniffing for us. *This*, I thought, *is what it's like for little fish cowering down deep among the reefs, sharks cruising between them and the bright surface.*

"You know what it's like?" Lennie said, watching the light shift up above us through the gaps in the floorboards. "It's like that dark angel Jacob wrestles in the Torah."

Schnabel gave Lennie the hairy eyeball. "So we're being hunted by an angel?" He chuffed.

"No," Lennie replied, "it's an alien. That's what it said the *Huldufólk* were at the end of *Investigation into the Invisible World COLON Huldufólk of Iceland DASH Elves, Ghosts, Sea Monsters, or Extraterrestrials QUESTION MARK.* The documentary says that the dark angel Jacob wrestles in Genesis Chapter thirty-two, verse twenty-two is the same kind of alien."

Anja was nodding, and I abruptly wanted to tear my hair out. Whatever soothing, soporific effect the house had, with its mellow light and curious books and comfy window seats, it didn't work down here. Down here, you just saw shit for what it was: a caged hunt put on for the pan-dimensional space-being equivalent of fat cats like Wall Street.

"Let's shake a tail feather," Schnabel said. "The coal bin is behind the furnace, and the coal chute will take us to the attic."

"Why not stay here?" Anja said. She was staring up, watching the shadow glide around, almost mesmerized. It seemed to sense it was near us but didn't get that we were a floor below it.

"The attic is . . . it's better," Schnabel said evasively. "'Cause it's further from the, ah, the 'bad elf.'"

I looked away from the ceiling to see him scrupulously *not* looking in my direction. I turned and discovered a doorway behind me, a plain, low opening in the far masonry wall. Beyond it was a shadowy room, maybe an old root cellar. I couldn't see much, but I could see, neatly arrayed across the floor in countless rows, many pairs of high-end sneakers: Air Force Ones, Jordans, a pair of classic white Superstar Adidas Originals, a couple other editions of LeBrons. Front and center was a pair of those pinky-purple Kobe 8 soccer-style sneakers with the glow-in-the-dark soles and Swoosh. There was no light in that room, but as my eyes adjusted to the dark I saw something hanging in there. Some*things*. Lots of somethings. I was reminded of the clotheslines my mom strung through the basement in the wintertime when I was a kid—how the pants and shirts moved a little in the draft, and how one time my older sister had called them "scarecrow skins" and it creeped me out so bad I couldn't set foot in the basement by myself again until I was in middle school.

But, of course, those weren't *scarecrow* skins hung on lines in the sneakerhead abattoir. They were human skins, most of them dark like mine, a few ghostly pale. Trophies. Or souvenirs? Or *hors d'oeuvres*?

Who the fuck knows? And how long do they know it, prior to ending up hanging in that room?

"Yeah," I said. "Let's make some distance between us and the bad elf."

And then I felt it, that tug in the guts Anja had described. Something was getting its grip on me. It was gentle and insinuating, like an infinitely patient child slowly bringing his cupped hands around a hapless toad. It *was* like a fishhook, deep in my guts. And it *was* like a net, looming over me despite being inside me. It was huge. It was delicate. It was maddening.

All I could hear was that high camera-flash noise, rattling my guts, vibrating every fluid in me. My vision narrowed to a tight tunnel, a darkness hashed with the parallel splinters of light that peeked through the floorboards. The alien angler had me, was reeling me in. But instead of pulling me *upward*, as a fisherman pulls a fish out of the water, it was pulling me *gutward*, and out of the known universe.

This was some mild version of what had been happening to Schnabel when we came in, and I wondered how he'd tolerated it, how he was so normal now. I'd never be normal again, never un-feel this feeling, never live in a universe where I was blissfully ignorant of the possibility of feeling this way.

I felt a pull—but this time an external pull, a

DAVID ERIK NELSON

mortal pull, at my middle. Anja was guiding me by my belt, like she was coaxing a dubious dog into the back seat of a small car. She eased my head down, the way cops do when they're forcing you into the back of a cruiser. It was the coal chute. I was in the coal chute. There was a slice of light ahead of me, and the creak of an iron door, and then the brightness of the Detroit autumn noon. I tumbled through, my heart light and free.

But instead of being outside in the dirt, I found myself crawling on hard boards under angled eaves.

"—we should've left him in the basement," Schnabel was saying. "Epstein's bad angel's got a hook in him; they're just paying out line."

"No," Anja said absently, "Glenn is fine. He just had, like, the anxiety attack, *já*, Glenn?"

"*Já*," I said, knowing it wasn't true. I was out from the looming shadow of the ancient sidereal fisherman, but Schnabel was right—deep in my gut I could still feel a little tug. Whatever it was that hunted in the house, it had me on the hook. "Yeah, I'm fine. I just get panic attacks."

"Really?" Lennie said. "You've never—"

"I get them at night," I snapped. I could feel little vibrations telegraphing along the fishline: patient fingers were testing the tension, trying to sound out how deep I'd dived.

"But it's lunchtime, Glenn."

"Not here it isn't," I said, indicating the dinner-plate-sized windows tucked into the gables at either end of the single large attic room. On one side the moon was full and bright, just peeking up over the lower edge of the window like one of those "Kilroy was here" grafittis. On the other there was a sickening overabundance of waxing and waning moons, overlapping each other like an insane bone-white biohazard sign. I don't even know if that's possible, for the moons of a single planet to be in different phases at the same time. I didn't really care, either: the angle of the pull in my guts was changing. Whatever had me on the hook was reeling me in, or reeling into me.

"How many ways out of here are there?" I asked, unable to keep my voice steady. The high-pitched camera whine was swelling, not just in my ears but permeating me, right through to the air in my lungs. The line in my gut tightened and there was a momentary tug that felt like I was being turned inside out—but a *different* kind of inside out. The insides of my body seemed likely to wind up enveloping the outside of the whole house, maybe the whole universe. I jerked in revulsion, my mouth twisting.

"The door we just came through dumps you out the laundry chute in the master bath," Schnabel said.

"Where does that laundry chute lead?" Anja asked.

"Dunno." Schnabel appraised Anja briefly, scanning her narrow shoulders and hips before shaking his head. "Too small for any of us to fit down. The tower is through there—" he pointed to a doorway, rosy dawn light spilling through "—but the windows are locked."

"Glenn has keys!" Lennie chimed as I lurched through the turret doorway, dragging against the pan-dimensional fishline in my guts.

The three windows were evenly spaced around the curved wall. Outside there was no Detroit, just a broad plane of wheat drenched in a bloody sunrise. The breeze pushed rolling waves across the fields of grain.

Windows number one and two were straight drops, three stories into the tall grass—and whatever might live down in the tall grass. But window number three would put us on the roof. It was the window I'd flopped through that first day.

Lennie looked out at the steeply pitched slates. "This doesn't seem like a great option, Glenn."

"It's better than the alternative," Schnabel said, for the first time acknowledging both his missing shoe and the fucked-up condition of his leg with the pant-leg pulled through it.

"They hunt us for our shoes?" Anja asked.

"The cowboys hunted out the buffalo for their tongues," Schnabel said. "It was a fucking industry. In a galaxy far, far away, maybe there's a big market for a pair of Adidas to hang on the wall."

Anja dropped to her knees and began methodically pulling the laces on her leather boots.

"I think they like 'em fresh," Schnabel told her, gentle as a grade-school teacher correcting a slow kid's spelling. "You know, with the feet still in 'em. Isn't like cowboys walked around just picking up any old tongues they found lying in the prairie."

"*Já, já, já,*" she muttered, still unlacing. "I do not care if they want the boots or do not want the boots; I just want to be less desirable to hunt, like a rhino with no horn, or a reindeer with mange."

"They, um, don't *just* want us for our shoes," Schnabel said. Anja froze. "You know, like how the buffalo hunters weren't *just* after tongues; they took the hides, too."

"Hides," she said. I nodded.

"I couldn't help but notice the collection they've got going down basement," Schnabel continued. "Good news for Washington: they seem to have plenty of dark meat on ice already. Bad news for us: there aren't many pale hides hanging down there. Yet."

"*Helvítis fokking fokk,*" Anja cursed, then began retying her shoes.

All of this washed over me. I was more interested in the windows—which were locked, but not with the nice Schlage SC4s; these were cheap little wafer locks, the kind you see on old desks and filing cabinets. I unclipped my keys from my belt. The bent, rusty old wafer key Fleischermann had given me fit perfectly and turned smoothly. I pushed the window open and it slid up easily. This struck me as off. Shouldn't it have lifted out? Hadn't it been top-hung, like a dog door, when I tumbled out of it after trying to come in through the back door?

There was some sort of monstrous storm brewing out there, clouds as mud-black as the grounds at the bottom of a cup of Turkish coffee, the distant mountains dark and jagged. At least it wasn't raining, I thought. Wet slate roofing tiles are slick as goose shit.

Right on cue, lightning cracked and the rain came in fat, greasy spatters. The wind whipped the tall grass savagely. I reflexively stepped away from the window, and then the bad elf gave a long, solid pull on the line, and I felt . . . I felt something . . . I think . . . It felt like my sternum pressed back and then passed through my spine, without passing through my skin. I could feel my heart beating outside my chest, fluttering against my left and right nipples, dead centered on each, but without touching the T-shirt that was already there. I tried to look down but the pressure was forcing my head back, white-washing my vision with scintillating stars, choking me. Then it released, and I slid back to normal.

Then there was a tug. Then it paid out some slack. I glanced back at Lennie and Anja and Schnabel. Their eyes were big as saucers.

"Glenn . . . ?" Anja began tentatively.

I shook my head. I didn't know what her question was, but I also didn't know what I was trying to communicate with that headshake. *No, I don't need help? No, I'm **not** OK?* Or just, *NO*, straight up, without predicate, a total refusal of everything that was happening to us there in the house.

I stepped back to the sill, prepared to hoist myself out the window, then froze.

"Come on, kid," Schnabel cajoled, "soonest begun, soonest done, just like Mom used to say."

You always smell a big storm like that—it smells like pennies. But this didn't smell like anything. And I didn't feel a lick of breeze.

A trap. It was a trap.

I dug into my pocket and came up with a beer bottle cap. God knows why I had it, but it was as good as anything. I flicked it out the window with my thumb, coin-toss style. Felt an awful pang doing it, like I was abandoning the poor little guy to fend for himself.

The others didn't notice, but that cap never hit the slates: instead, it clattered down the long chimney, all the way to the basement.

I eased the window back down and relocked it. The key hung up for a second as I was doing so. That was the worst part, although I can't say why. I jiggled it loose, as gently as a man defusing a bomb, and returned the key ring safely to my belt.

"We can't get out this way," I heard myself say. "It's a trap. When I picked the locks that first day, the house wouldn't let me in—some sorta child-safe cap, to keep out lookie-loos and worthless prey. The way little fish can swim right through a lobster pot. But unlock the doors proper and the trap is set. Anja and I were only able to saunter out yesterday because we left the door hanging open. The trap hadn't sprung."

Schnabel was nodding the way real estate guys do when you are explaining that there's a problem, and this is what it's gonna cost to fix it.

"Got it: use the key to climb out, we're just gonna

tumble right back in the cellar door or some shit. It's a tease."

"It is a cruel trap," Anja lamented.

Schnabel shook his head, annoyed. "Then just don't use the fucking key, dumbass," he said. "You're a fully bonded fucking locksmith, Washington."

"Glenn has an intermediate certificate from the Associated Locksmiths of America!" Lennie added. No one acknowledged him. He had to shout to be heard over the singing high-pitched tone, which was growing louder and yet more diffuse, permeating us. The hunter was approaching.

My lips were numb as I spoke. "My picks are in the glove box." I always keep them in my glove box. It doesn't pay to be a black man wandering around with "burglar's tools" on his person.

"But not your snowman," Lennie shouted matter-of-factly. Schnabel and Anja turned to look at him. "You lost it when you were on the roof, and then found it in the yard, and then put it in the inside pocket of your jacket, where you always put things and then forget you put them and then we end up looking all over for them because things get lost in that pocket because it's so deep, like the time you thought the waitress didn't bring back your ATM card at China King."

I shoved my hand into the deep inner pocket and was promptly stabbed between my first two fingers by my missing tension wrench. The snowman was wedged beneath it. I drew them out, slid the tension wrench into the lock, and applied the slightest pressure; one rake with the snowman and the window was freely banging against its frame, like a dog door in a gale. I pushed it out and everything was still the same—steeply pitched slates, lashing, greasy storm—but this time I could smell it, copper and gunpowder and cinnamon. The wind whipped my jacket around like a flag. I flung myself through the little window—anything was better than being in there—but was not drenched by the sheeting rain. Instead I rolled down the front steps like Buster Keaton and smacked my head on the frost-heaved walkway pavers. I came to rest flat on my back in the autumn-afternoon sunshine, staring up at the eaves and the clear blue sky beyond.

The house had rejected me. I'd escaped. We'd escaped.

I rolled my head and squinted into the shadowy entryway alcove. Lennie and Schnabel were already out. Lennie hunched on the bottom step with his hands hanging off his knees. Schnabel stood tall at the edge of the top step, despite his warped leg, arms relaxed at his sides, head back, taking in the crisp air like a dog snorting through the gap at the top of a car window.

"This," he sighed, his eyes closed, "has been quite enlightening." He moseyed down the steps and stood in the yard, soaking up the free air and sunshine.

Anja ducked out the darkened doorway like a woman slipping through a beaded curtain. She jogged down the steps, stepped over my sprawled legs, and continued down the path.

I dragged myself up, wincing at the twinges in my back, elbows, and hips.

"Where you headed?" I asked.

"Home," she said without breaking stride. Her tone suggested that "home" didn't mean whatever gutter-chic hipster apartment she shared with Ms. Thang who'd called my cell phone earlier.

"We all just experienced a sorta big thing," I called. "Maybe we should debrief? Have a coffee or a beer and chat?"

She kept walking.

"You need a lift?" I practically shouted. She vaulted the gate without missing a beat and continued down the block, head high, boots tapping smartly on the concrete, a woman with places to go and people to see.

Without a doubt, she was the only one of us who learned whatever valuable lesson there was to glean from this experience.

I turned back to the house and wasn't shocked to see that she'd firmly closed the door behind her on the way out. No loose ends this time. Sharp lady.

Except . . .

Except for that it was pretty obvious that locking up this gun wasn't nearly good enough to keep anyone from getting shot in the foot. I thought of all those sneakers in the basement, of all the sneakerheads they'd been sawed off. I thought of the trans-dimensional alien whoevers that paid good gold-pressed latinum for the opportunity to come to this canned hunt, and the earthling mutherfuckers who kept the hunt stocked to serve their own ends. A gun locker keeps you safe from everyone except the murderous fuckers with the keys to the lock.

"What are we gonna do about this place, Lennie?"

He looked up and set his mouth with concentration.

"Weeellll," he drawled nasally, "the Original Butcher Man, of blessed memory, he would've burned it." He leaned out and twisted around to appraise the house. I was dubious. Lennie was not. "He told me once that these old ones are all balloon constructed. That means there's a wood frame for the outside walls, and all the weight is on that." It occurred to me then that the Fleischermanns' long commitment to Lennie had hardly been an act of simple charity. Lennie, in his own special way, was a very useful dude. "You set a fire in the basement, beneath the front stairs—good dry wood—and it spreads quick. Once it's in the walls—fircmen call it 'fully involved'—the walls can't hold the weight. The house folds up like a card table. Quick. Firemen won't even try and put it out 'cause it's too risky. They just contain it." He worked his mouth as though doing math in his head. "But getting into the basement here is tricky, because none of the stairs go like you think. It might take too long to get out." He paused. "That'd be bad. I guess instead we could set a fire on the main staircase, along the wall. But first bust up the plaster so that the fire can get in." Lennie nodded. "That's the best. That's how the Original Butcher Man would do it. There's diesel in the truck, yeah?"

"No," I said, my mind elsewhere. "Just two-cycle, for the chainsaw and weed-whip." I didn't like that phrase, *the house folds up like a card table*. Didn't like the images it conjured.

Lennie was frowning shaking his head. "Two-cycle is no good. It's too fumy. Sometimes gasoline won't catch, other times it explodes. We need something heavy, like diesel or paint thinner."

"We've got paint thinner." I imagined what the house might be like when it burned. A fire has to draw in air to thrive, but where would that air come from? Would it suck in through the open front door? Good old Detroit air, cleaner every day because there's hardly any industry left. Or would it be the air from that dark, jagged landscape? Or from one of the countless other worlds with their countless moons and bright, foreign stars? What if the fire spread? This neighborhood was just rubble on quarter-acre lots, basically fire-proof. But what about over there? What about the fields of grain outside the attic windows? How long would all that burn, and what would happen if the wind changed direction and the smoke from those eldritch wildfires blew into our fair city?

I'd seen rats and roaches come boiling out of burning houses here in the D. What might flee the crooked house?

But that was all rationalization. The true truth was that the architect in me, that expensively, exquis-itely trained art-engineer, recoiled in disgust at the very idea of destroying the house. Even knowing what I knew. None of these guys—not Fleischer-mann, not his dad, none of the Schnabels or Epsteins—were architects. They were all develop-ers, which means builders, but also means tearer-downers. They weren't trained like me, and they had no interest in being trained like me.

And so they didn't know what I did: that it would be wrong, fundamentally wrong, to destroy the house. The house might be dangerous, even vicious, but it was also lovely, and it's wrong to kill a thing—especially something so graceful and strange—if you can render it safe and leave it intact.

"Naw," I said. "I don't like the idea of burning her."

"Me either," Schnabel said, his voice flat and cold as iron plate.

"I don't like the idea of opening those doors again, either," I went on. "We've got a BernzOmatic in the toolbox—"

"Glenn?" Lennie whispered.

"Did we ever get more plumbing solder?" I asked Lennie. Something tapped my shoulder. I turned, and Schnabel pressed the deadly little Five-SeveN gently to the tip of my nose. His finger was resting on the trigger.

"This is my house," he said, holding out his free hand, palm up. "And it's a very, very, very fine house. Keys?" I discovered that my hands had already risen of their own volition. One eased down to my belt, unclipped my half-pound key ring, and handed it over. Schnabel scowled and handed it back.

"Jesus, this isn't a stickup; take my keys off your keys and give them to me." I wrestled with the split ring a little and did as he asked. He finally holstered his gun, then went back up the front steps and checked to be sure his front door was locked.

"Swell. You assholes give me a ride back to my office. And, before you ask, I don't wanna do a fucking *kaffeeklatsch* with you either, Washington." He looked at his watch, then at the sun in the sky, then back at his watch. "Unbelievable. Not even two p.m."

"I'd get coffee with you, Glenn," Lennie said earnestly, "but me and my mom and dad are going to watch the Lions play the Vikings on TV."

We three piled into the cab of the S-10, Lennie crammed into the middle seat. We didn't talk much, instead listening to NPR. The program changed and the announcer introduced himself as "Glynn Washington." Lennie asked if we were related, I said that yeah, we were cousins. Lennie was agog, and Schnabel chuckled at me clowning on the dimwit.

The thing is, I wasn't clowning on Lennie: me and

that Glynn Washington actually *are* cousins. It's a funny little universe, right?

When I dropped Schnabel off, he turned back, stood in the door of the truck, and once again gave me the once over.

"I've got some things to straighten out today," he said. "People to see. But I'll be in touch. I need a better class of employee. A smart guy like you." He closed the door gently, and I headed back toward Detroit, intent on dropping Lennie off on the way. When we pulled up in front of his parents' nice little suburban split-level brick ranch, I finally broached the subject.

"I've been thinking about quitting," I said. "Doing something for myself instead of being a contractor doing piddlyshit for crooked cats."

Lennie nodded. "That's good. Dick Schnabel is right: you're better than this job. You've got a Bachelors of Architecture from the University of Michigan, Ann Arbor, home of the Wolverines, and also studied at the Cranbrook Academy of Art, which is renowned for its architecture in the Arts and Crafts, Swedish Modern, and Art Deco styles."

"You wanna do that new thing with me? I mean,

you're better than the Fleischermanns' crooked shit, too."

Lennie scowled. "These are my family, Glenn. I'm not better than my family."

I nodded. You can't really save anyone, right? Can't straighten a dog's leg; you'll just make all parties miserable by trying.

"But I'll miss working with you," Lennie added. "You're a solid dude."

"You're a solid dude, too." We bumped fists. And that was that.

I drove home and spent the next few hours working on the walls of my own house in that blurry border region inexplicably dividing Mexican Village from Mexicantown—as though anyone who isn't trying to sell or rent a property there could give a shit about the difference. But that's urban development: every place needs a name. That's what makes it a place.

My walls are plaster and lath backed with horse-hair, and I was redoing them just exactly that way; not with drywall, or even with modern plaster and that reinforcing wire. I was doing it right. Dead level and plumb, perfectly smooth and flat, not a crooked corner in the whole place. No one would ever notice or care—authentic plaster walls ain't granite countertops. But I cared. I'd always know I'd done it right. That was suddenly super-duper existentially important to me.

I spent the day working on my walls and not particularly thinking about anything, but when the sun started to tip over toward the rooftops, I rinsed off my tools and headed back out to the crooked house.

It looked just the same, which surprised me. I don't know what I'd expected—some concrete sign, I guess, of the bad things that happened in there, the bad things that came to the house to hunt. But none of that was evident. It was just the house, standing handsome—if a touch crooked—at the top of its little rubble hillock. The only hint was something subtle and inexpressible: in contrast to all the other houses I'd worked on for the Fleischermanns over the years, this one didn't *feel* vacant. Maybe briefly untenanted, but not *abandoned*. This house kept itself occupied.

I started with the back door: painted the keyhole with some flux, sparked the BernzOmatic propane torch, and patiently heated that nice Schlage plug until it went dusky. When I nuzzled the tip of the solder to the keyhole, it immediately relaxed into the lock and ran back in, down between the pins, hopelessly bunging it.

Circling back around the other side, I found a bulkhead cellar door with a halfway decent locking hasp and bunged that, too. It wasn't until I'd finished with the front door that the knot I'd had in my guts since my first foray into the joint with Anja finally loosened.

I cupped my hands against all those pretty little diamond panes for one last gander into that pristine, Pewabic-tiled lobster trap. And there was Cop A, dazed and staring right back at me. I jerked away, kicking over the torch, then scrambled to grab it before its hot tip could start trouble. Cop A didn't hear or see any of this, and when I thought about it, that made sense: he was locked in the house. Whatever he was seeing through those windows—maybe crescent moons as numerous as the stars, or amber waves of grain—it sure as hell wasn't me.

Locked in the house.

The idea was revolting, and without thinking I blindly reached out to open the door for him. I got a burn for my troubles.

Cop A stepped back from the glass, revealing Cop B—Officer Washington, no relation—tucked under one of the green reading lamps. Both cops looked bad: someone had worked them over pretty thoroughly. Cop B's ears were uneven. A trickle of blood ran down the side of his neck, darkening his collar. The shoulder seam on his shirt was split, exposing a clean, white swath of undershirt. But none of that troubled him: he stooped to catch the best light under the dim lamp, a book in hand, furiously devouring the pages. I could just make out the title, done in gold foil on the dark blue hardback. It was *The International Jew and Protocols of the Elders of R'lyeh*, translation by Henry Ford.

Cop A continued pacing the front hall. His lip was split, his right eye swollen shut, his nose stuffed with a couple wads of Kleenex. Back and forth he paced, like a caged panther. Neither cop had his cop utility belt, with its keys and batons and Tasers and pistols and pepper spray and whatever. Grotesquely, both had been stripped of their sensible black cop shoes and were instead wearing garish, brand-new top-end Nikes, the kinds coveted by corner boys and sneakerheads.

I backed away from the door. The locks were bunged and, even if they hadn't been, I didn't have keys any more. Schnabel was the only man in the world with keys to the crooked house, and it isn't like he intended to let the cops back out once he'd shoved them in. Their association with Schnabel Asset Group and all of its subsidiaries had been terminated.

Schnabel.

The name sounded like the rasp and ratchet of someone running the slide on a pricy little pistol.

There was nothing I could do for them. There was nothing *anyone* could do for them. They were completely and totally fucked.

And that was on me. I hadn't built the place, I hadn't shoved them in—shit, I hadn't made all these crooked mutherfuckers crooked to begin with—but I'd drawn them all together, like some extra-special bumblefuck bait, with my perfect ratio of not-sticking-with-shit to not-leaving-weird-enough-alone.

I backed away from the door but still clearly saw the jagged, oily shadow-thing unwind from thin air. It slid between the two cops, occluding Cop B, who never even glanced up from his book. Cop A threw himself against the front door, fists hammering what should have been delicate panes, mouth twisted in a silent scream. The dark angel began folding Cop A up, and I couldn't stand another second of it.

I spun and sprinted down the uneven front walk. The pavers seemed to heave beneath my feet, like a rotting rope bridge crumbling away into an abyss. I stole a glance over my shoulder and saw the house distort and loom and judder, like a net being drawn tight.

I leapt down the walk, hitting the chain link gate hard enough to knock my snot loose and fill my head with effervescent stars. I hauled my ass over the gate, came down painfully on the concrete, rolled off onto the broken asphalt, and bounced to my feet, shoulders hunched. I whipped around to get a bead on the fucking house, terrified it was lunging for the kill.

But it wasn't there.

The whole *lot* wasn't there: no rubble. No hill. No nothing. Just a chain link gate pointlessly mounted on a blank piece of sidewalk between two adjacent wrecks that had somehow snugged together. The addresses on the sagging, beat-down mailboxes skipped four numbers instead of just two.

The house hadn't been looming or lunging; it had been folding up, like a patio umbrella that's done for the season. Clear enough what happened, I suppose: with their canned hunt queered, there was no sense sticking around. The alien bad elves had folded up their hunters' blind and gone home.

Or, at least, that's what I hoped.

CODA

FOR A GUY I'd never heard of before, Dick Schnabel proved harder to avoid than you'd think. Haven't seen the gimpy sonofabitch since, but his office was blowing up my phone, so I broke contract and got a new number. It rang a call from "Schnabel Properties" while I was still standing in the parking lot. Ditched it, bought a pay-by-the-minute no-contract phone at a liquor store, and two days later Schnabel called that, too. FedEx just delivered a "guaranteed anonymous burner" I bought online from some German who only accepted goddamn Bitcoin. That hasn't rung yet, but who knows what tomorrow will bring?

I'm not really sweating it, though. Believe it or not, being on that real estate gangster's speed dial isn't my biggest worry.

Here's my big worry: the heartburn I've had all week, since I "escaped" the crooked house? It ain't heartburn. It's lower than heartburn, and heartburn, it *burns*—it doesn't *pull*.

Walking all over town, doing my daily, I feel myself pivoting around that inside-out pull, like a fish dragging a slack line. Maybe slack because it's broken? Maybe slack because the angler is still paying out line, letting the fish tire himself?

I don't know.

I don't know, and you don't care. It's S.E.P. to you. Your problem, as an independent real estate broker, is that you gotta live on sales commissions. Bad news: I ain't looking to buy. Good news: I've got this li'l green portrait of Ben Franklin, and it is *heavy*. I'm just gonna rest it on your desk while you take a second to query the Multiple Listing Service for every property associated with an architect named "Quintus Teal." Print out the sheets, hand 'em over, and I'll be so excited, I'll totally forget that I was resting this Benjamin here and be on my merry way. You, meanwhile, will be so excited by your good fortune that you'll entirely forget we ever met or you ever heard of such an architect—

especially if someone from "Schnabel Properties" shows interest.

I *don't* know how many Quintus Teal properties you'll find. Just one? Maybe a few? Maybe dozens? But I *do* know this: hunters and fishermen—be they mundane or sidereal—are tenacious mutherfuckers, serious dudes of the first order. They don't give up because the quarry gets scarce. Shit, that's part of the game. They don't quit and go home; they set up in another neck of the woods.

And I also know this: I can be a fish, mindlessly running until the line goes taught and pulls him up out of the Universe into God knows what.

Or I can go house hunting.

ABOUT THE AUTHOR

David Erik Nelson is an award-winning science-fiction/horror author and essayist who has become increasingly aware that he's "that unsavory character" in other people's anecdotes. His stories have appeared in *Asimov's*, the *Magazine of Fantasy & Science Fiction*, *Pseudopod*, *The Best Horror of the Year*, and elsewhere. In addition to writing stories about time travel, sex robots, haunted dogs, and carnivorous lights, he also writes non-fiction about synthesizers, guns, cyborg cockroaches, and Miss America.

• Find him at davideriknelson.com or twitter.com/squidaveo

• Find free fiction at davideriknelson.com/FreeFiction

Nicholas Grunas created the cover art. Find more of his work online at https://www.facebook.com/djjustnick and https://pixels.com/artists/djjustnick08

Made in the USA
Monee, IL
19 December 2019